It was futile. The car was nearly upon them...

Abruptly, Beckett grabbed Laney's arm and pulled her to the side.

They watched as the car continued straight ahead and smashed front first into the rear of their van. Glass spewed in all directions. Metal crumpled with a squeal that drowned out Laney's scream.

They were alive. She hugged herself in disbelief, but Beckett was urging her up.

"Keep going. Don't stop."

Come on.

le pitch

n. She houlder recked teeth

las

Dana Mentink is a nationally bestselling author. She has been honored to win two Carol Awards, a HOLT Medallion and an RT Reviewers' Choice Best Book Award. She's authored more than thirty novels to date for Love Inspired Suspense and Harlequin Heartwarming. Dana loves feedback from her readers. Contact her at danamentink.com.

Books by Dana Mentink

Love Inspired Suspense

Desert Justice
Framed in Death Valley

True Blue K-9 Unit: Brooklyn
Cold Case Pursuit

True Blue K-9 Unit
Shield of Protection
Act of Valor

Roughwater Ranch Cowboys
Danger on the Ranch
Deadly Christmas Pretense
Cold Case Connection
Secrets Resurfaced

Gold Country Cowboys
Cowboy Christmas Guardian
Treacherous Trails
Cowboy Bodyguard
Lost Christmas Memories

Visit the Author Profile page at Harlequin.com for more titles.

FRAMED IN DEATH VALLEY

DANA MENTINK

LOVE INSPIRED SUSPENSE

INSPIRATIONAL ROMANCE

LOVE INSPIRED® SUSPENSE
INSPIRATIONAL ROMANCE

ISBN-13: 978-1-335-58111-2

Framed in Death Valley

Copyright © 2021 by Dana Mentink

For questions and comments about the quality of this book, please contact us
at CustomerService@Harlequin.com.

Love Inspired
22 Adelaide St. West, 40th Floor
Toronto, Ontario M5H 4E3, Canada
www.Harlequin.com

Printed in U.S.A.

There is therefore now no condemnation to them
which are in Christ Jesus, who walk not after the flesh,
but after the Spirit.
–*Romans* 8:1

For Ann, my golden-hearted friend
who has given so much to so many.

ONE

Beckett Duke hunched in the passenger seat, avoiding the narrowing gaze of the man who'd given him a lift.

The radio news reporter delivered the words impassively, but they hit like bombs. "The murder case against local firefighter Beckett Duke was dismissed due to improper police procedure. Duke was released from jail this morning, according to Inyo County's DA's office. He was awaiting trial for the murder of Pauline Sanderson, a forty-two-year-old nurse visiting Death Valley National Park. Her body was found on the grounds of the Hotsprings Hotel."

The man behind the wheel squinted suddenly, his gaze sliding from the radio to

Beckett as he put the thing together in his mind. Beckett pulled his baseball cap down farther on his brow, but the damage was already done.

"My vision ain't so good anymore and you look different without your beard. If I'da known who you were," the man growled, "I might have run you down instead of given you a lift. Get out."

Though they were still more than a mile from the Hotsprings Hotel and the late-October temperatures were cracking the ninety-degree mark, Beckett did as he was told, struggling to eject his six-foot-four frame from the front seat. The sun beat down on him with hammer blows.

Before he drove off, the man rolled down his window. "You got some nerve comin' back here, Beckett Duke. I hope you get what's coming to you."

Beckett didn't reply, just stood there in the ferocious heat, jaw tight as the man delivered the final blow. "You've always been a monster," he added, before leaving Beckett in a cloud of exhaust.

Monster, a title he'd earned in high school. Even now, at age forty-three, he could remember the exact moment when he'd executed the throw in the wrestling match. But something had gone wrong. He'd been too quick, too forceful. He heard the snap of his opponent's neck, instant collapse, moaning. The hush in that shocked high school auditorium echoed louder in his memory than the aftermath of boos and shouted insults that would follow. Beckett had caused a head injury that blinded a young man with a brilliant future ahead, a full-ride scholarship to an Ivy League school. One moment had ruined both their lives.

Out of that terrible event came the parade of accusations, blame and paralyzing self-doubt. Hadn't he realized that Dan Wheatly was not confident? That he hadn't been fully ready for Beckett's overeager attack?

Bully.

Animal.

Monster.

He swiped a hand across his sweating brow. That was twenty-six years ago. It had no bearing on his current situation, which was dire enough. The message had been delivered to him in jail three days before, in the form of punches that blackened his eye and busted his lip, kicks that bruised his ribs, while the other inmates cheered and hooted.

How does it feel, tough guy? The beating hadn't scared him nearly as bad as the whisper in his ear from the two prisoners who held him down and pummeled him. *Kenny is going to kill you for what you did to his sister.* It wasn't a threat, but a promise. Paroled felon Kenny Sanderson intended to kill him. That he could accept. His life was over anyway, his reputation in tatters, his heart so numb it could have been replaced by a hunk of solid stone. It was the second part of the message that reverberated in his ears like a scream echoing along a desert canyon.

And your wife too.

Laney. They'd been married exactly

thirty-seven days before he'd found Pauline Sanderson's body. On that hideous morning he'd discovered her dumped in a wooded culvert on hotel property, not a stone's throw from Death Valley National Park. Pauline, his former high school flame, had been looking for him—left a message, in fact.

I have to talk to you. Urgent.

He should have told Laney. No secrets, they'd agreed. Nothing should cloud the absolute joy of their unlikely marriage, not the twelve-year age difference, not the infertility she could still not accept, not the hard work of running his family's hotel in the middle of the most hostile environment in the world. Nothing could ever have separated them, short of murder. As the situation snowballed, the only way to save her from the hatred and stain of being married to the most reviled man in Furnace Falls was a divorce. His jailhouse beating courtesy of Kenny had only confirmed that. The divorce would give her a future and keep her safe. It was her one chance, and it nearly killed him to contact the lawyer.

Yet here he was, in the same disheveled clothes he'd been wearing when he'd been remanded to the county jail, jeans, a Furnace Falls Fire Department T-shirt and a pair of steel-toed boots, squinting at the entrance to the Hotsprings Hotel.

The squat wood-paneled front office faced a view of the mountains. The smell of slow-cooked brisket beckoned. Herm Devendorf would have started the big iron pot simmering that morning for the dinner service. His mouth watered.

The hotel had been his home away from home since he was eight years old and his mother passed of cancer, helping out his father, who'd later deeded him the place. His cousin Jude used to swim in the pool with him when they were kids. They'd roam the sun-soaked acres of salt flats and desert scrub and then plunge into the pool until hunger drove them out. How times changed. Now Jude was a cop who hadn't offered a word of support when Beckett had been arrested. No surprise there. Jude's animosity spanned into the past to that day when Beckett had blinded Dan, Jude's best friend, in that wrestling ring.

"You can do this," he told himself. Heart thumping, he forced his legs to carry him toward the front. The driveway led to the registration office. Nearby he saw the hotel shuttle parked in a discreet spot.

Then Laney walked out the front door, offering that bright smile that he dreamed about to a visitor on the porch. He forgot everything but the pain arcing straight to his core. Her long honey-colored hair was pulled into a high ponytail that cascaded down her shoulders over a loose-fitting T-shirt. Leggings hugged her trim calves.

Laney. His Laney. She appeared tired as she moved toward the hotel van. She'd always been petite and delicate, her wrists so small he'd marveled at how he could wrap his thumb and forefinger completely around. And the smallest feet, she could almost fit two of them into one of his big old clodhoppers.

As she opened the driver's-side door, her scream cut the air and she stumbled back.

In spite of the searing heat, his body went cold. Had Kenny Sanderson already arrived to make good on his threats?

"Please, God," he said, as he began to sprint. "Don't let me be too late."

Laney tumbled backward, shock still ripping through her. There in the front seat she could see the snake clearly, a buff-colored body with darker blotches and a wedge-shaped head. Its forked tongue sampled the air. The little rattles vibrated their warning.

If she hadn't been paying attention, she might have sat right down on the venomous creature. She swallowed against a suddenly dry throat, frozen, staring into the gleaming eyes of the viper.

The rational side of her brain told her it was a Mojave Desert Sidewinder, and its bite, contrary to belief, was not fatal. Still, the fear seized control of her mind; she could not be bitten by this rattler, not now.

She told herself to freeze and slowly, ever so slowly, back away. It was too late. Should she try to reach out for the door or run? But the viper had a striking distance measuring a third of its body.

Those fangs...the fear...

The snake reared forward. Her scream was high and shrill as she braced for a bite. Instinct caused her to jerk up her hand to shield herself. Then, as if she were dreaming, Beckett was there. He dived into her field of vision and kicked the car door closed.

She sank to her knees, unable to still her trembling as she heard the sound of the fangs striking the inside of the van door. Her whole body shook. The snake was one thing; having Beckett show up was just as shocking.

Beckett knelt next to her and grasped her arm. "Did it bite you?"

"No. I'm fine. It just scared me, is all." She pushed the words out.

His fingers rested on her wrist for a moment. "You're shaking."

She detached herself from his touch, unable to tear her gaze from him. "I'm okay." It was a mantra she'd been repeating to herself since the day Pauline Sanderson's body had been found on the property and all her dreams had dried up and blown away. No, not quite then. She'd still believed with all her heart that she and Beckett would be together forever, for better or worse, and she'd continued believing that right up until the divorce papers arrived. "I'm really okay," she repeated, as if saying it aloud would make it somehow true. Shading her eyes, she stared. "What are you doing here?"

She'd heard he was being released, but she hadn't thought he'd show up at the hotel. She got to her feet so quickly she swayed. Beckett steadied her, but she had to bend over until the dizziness subsided. Emotions rampaged through her from relief that he was free, disbelief that he'd chosen to return, but eclipsing all was the tearing sadness in her heart in the place where love used to be.

Beckett Duke, the man she thought would be her soul mate forever, was now just a stranger like all the rest of the people who paraded on and off the hotel property. She swallowed a lump in her throat.

He looked different: his tall frame thinner. His face was gaunt, his dark hair cut prison short. Her breath caught at the damage to his face: blackened eye, a cut across the bridge of his nose. What happened? she wondered, but she would not ask.

"Laney," he said, breathing fast from his run. "Are you sure you're not hurt?"

The sheer irony of the question. She blinked, staring, unable to process. How could he even ask it? "I told you I'm okay, but you haven't explained what you're doing here." She couldn't stop the bitterness from spilling out. "Checking to see if I signed the divorce papers yet?"

The word *divorce* burned like poison in her mouth. In fact, the papers still sat in her desk drawer, waiting for her signature, a scrawled name that would mean an end to a relationship she'd thought was God ordained. Her head began to pound.

Jude Duke pulled up in his patrol car, stepped out and hustled over. He shot Beckett a hostile glare, the sun glinting off his sheriff's badge. He was a few inches shorter than Beckett, his eyes hazel to Beckett's brown. "Mom wanted me to bring you some jam, Laney." He must have seen the distress on her face because he asked, "What happened?"

Beckett explained about the snake.

"Are you bitten?" Jude asked.

Laney shook her head, hoping her voice sounded steady. "I brought supplies back from the park for one of the guests. The snake must have crawled into his pack before we loaded it in the back." Was she really calmly explaining things in front of her soon-to-be-former husband?

Jude nodded. "Snake hitchhiked out of the park, huh? I'll call animal control." He stepped away to speak into his radio.

Beckett kept those chocolate eyes on her until she thought she would scream.

They were not the same eyes she remembered. They were harder, duller and missing something she could not identify. "I need to talk to you, Laney. Privately," he said.

Oh, how she'd wanted to talk, begged him through letters and stilted jail phone conversations. She would have done anything to talk to Beckett and make him see she believed in him no matter what, that she'd stand by him every day of his life. Now it was too late. She shook her head, willing herself to return his gaze. "You made it clear what you wanted, Beck. There's nothing more to say."

The muscles in his throat worked. "This is important. You're in danger."

She could not help darting a look at him then. "What?"

His expression was something she'd never seen in him before, something wild and desperate. In danger? Beckett was many things, but he was not a murderer, of that she was dead certain. Someone else had killed Pauline Sanderson.

A killer...the real monster...had never been caught, though no one would ever believe it. The murderer was undoubtedly long gone, had probably left the tiny town of Furnace Falls far behind. There was no criminal on the loose here. Was there?

Beckett felt Jude's hard stare as he finished his radio conversation and rejoined them, handing Laney a jar of jam. He squared off with Beckett. The distrust radiated off him in palpable waves. Beckett had learned the hard way that Jude was a cop first and a cousin second. As the evidence had piled up against Beckett after Pauline's body was found, Jude had put him squarely in the enemy camp.

"You haven't explained why you're here," Jude said.

"I need to talk to my wife."

He arched an eyebrow. "She doesn't seem at all eager to talk to you, now that you served her with divorce papers. Classy act to do that to her."

Beckett would have vented his simmering rage if Laney hadn't been there. She wrapped her arms around herself and pressed her lips together. She was pale underneath the freckles, perhaps from the shock of seeing him, the unforgiving Death Valley sun, the snake or a combination of all three. He didn't want to upset her any more. He bit back his ire.

Jude bobbed his chin. "Why don't you go find a place in town to stay if you must?"

Laney was like a sister to Jude and he understood his cousin's protectiveness, but Laney was Beckett's to take care of— for a while longer, anyway. He fisted his hands, teeth grinding together. "This is still my family's land."

And legally it was, since they had not yet finished the process of transitioning it to joint property when he was arrested. Nothing had been finished, nothing at all, before Pauline was murdered. He wondered if it ever would be. "I won't stay long."

"Better if you didn't stay at all, but I

can't force you to leave. I'm asking you to think about Laney."

"I am," he snapped. "I have to talk to her, that's all. And there's something you need to know too, as a cop, so you can get some plans in place."

Jude's shoulders tensed. "You just stroll back into town and start telling me how to do my job? You got some nerve. The only reason you're out is because one of my officers mishandled evidence and broke the chain of custody. We messed up. That doesn't mean you deserve to be a free man."

"I am going inside," Laney said suddenly, drawing their attention. "Jude, please let me know when the snake's taken care of."

She left them there staring at each other. When she passed, Beckett thought he noticed her blinking back tears.

As he went after her, he heard Jude's low remark, cold and guttural. "Haven't you hurt her enough?"

Beckett did not acknowledge Jude's

comment. Doing so might crack through the infinitesimally thin sheet of glass that kept him from complete despair. The other barriers had shattered already. He was not sure how his fragile protection would hold up walking back into the cozy dining hall after Laney, but there was no other option. In order to protect her, he'd have to add more pain, and he hated himself for that. The injustice of it smacked him. God had been punishing Beckett since he was that brash seventeen-year-old wrestler, but surely Laney did not deserve to share in it.

He needed to keep her safe from Kenny. The divorce was still the only answer.

TWO

When Beckett pushed through the screen door into the rustic dining hall, he found the place unchanged. He was greeted by dark woods, the enormous stone fireplace and long family-style tables that had been there since Beckett's father bought the hotel and grounds. He breathed it all in with mixed pain and pleasure, the aroma of the place that used to be home. His eyes sought the wooden shelf he'd built where there had been a silver-framed picture of him and Laney on their wedding day. The photo had been removed. It probably brought Laney a boatload of pain looking at the man who she'd thought had been her life partner. Little did she know he'd be jailed less than two months after their wedding and filing for divorce in four.

A dog with a sausage-shaped body scurried to him, rising up on arthritic hind legs to paw at his shins. He was a weird conglomerate of dachshund, Chihuahua and something fuzzier. Smiling, he took a knee. "Hey, Admiral. Have you been helping your mama?" His mama was and always would be Laney, the primary object of his adoration. He scratched behind the dog's fox-like ears until the bulging brown eyes glazed and a pink tongue unrolled through the spot where a missing front tooth should be.

He flashed back to the day he'd run into Pete Parson, the town vet, guzzling coffee in the local java joint, grumbling how a visitor through town had taken their ill senior dog to the vet and abandoned him there rather than foot the bill. Pete was already the owner of five dogs and three cats. The softhearted vet was struggling with the decision to euthanize the unwanted animal. Beckett had spoken about it at the hotel, and Laney, a part-time housekeeper, overheard. She promptly burst into tears, phoned the vet and begged him to keep the dog safe until she could earn the money to pay the bill and adopt him. His heart throbbed, remembering how she was halfway through a double shift scrubbing floors at the hotel when Beckett presented her with the dog and a fully paid vet bill.

Laney had again begun to cry and he realized he'd never known such a beautiful woman both inside and out. She'd looked at Beckett like he was a hero, and he'd never forgotten it.

"His new name is Admiral Nelson," she'd announced later as she carefully applied drops to the dog's only working eye. "A thirteen-year-old dog should have a dignified name, don't you think? I was reading about the real admiral's naval victories in a book Aunt Kitty gave me. The human Admiral Nelson had only one working eye too," she'd said, kissing the dog on his nose.

Both Beckett and the dog lost their hearts to Laney Holland right around then. He gave the dog a final pat. At least Admiral would never abandon Laney. As he straightened, he noted a middle-aged woman in the corner with a book in her hand, her hair braided into a long dark column down her back.

When she saw he'd noticed her, she dropped her attention back to the open book. There was something odd about her. His instincts prickled. Was she simply curious about a newcomer? Or did she believe the town gossip about who he was...the monster returned to his killing grounds?

Another theory presented itself. A sliver of cold pierced his innards. Had Kenny sent an advance team? Perhaps this woman had been the one to put a snake in the van on Kenny's orders?

Paranoia or reasonable suspicion? He didn't know anymore. The sun blazed through the front window, and the old air conditioner fought to keep up. He recalled the day in June when his life exploded.

The dining hall had been similarly empty then as well; only a few guests were brave enough to hazard Death Valley in late spring. He'd found the folded note on the bulletin board, pinned there with his name on the front. He'd gotten up earlier than usual that day to surprise Laney with her favorite doughnut from a shop in town. Chocolate old-fashioned. He'd spotted the note on his way into the kitchen.

I have to talk to you. Urgent. Come as soon as you can to the creek.—Pauline.

What he'd found at that creek, which had been dry for months, was Pauline Sanderson's body, throat ringed with bruises, back of her skull oozing blood. He'd tried CPR, called for help and stayed with her. As he sat next to her body, part of him knew nothing would ever be the same. About that, he'd been right.

Why had Pauline left him the note?

Why hadn't he told his wife where he was going?

He had no answers for the police.

He had no explanations either for how

Pauline's bloody sweater got into the front seat of his vehicle.

The woman sipped her coffee. Avoiding his gaze? It occurred to him just then that it had been a very long time since she'd turned a page. She stood, closing her book, and left.

Was she a threat or an innocent tourist? He simply could not tell.

Figure it out, Beckett. Laney's life might depend on it.

Don't you cry, Laney, do you hear me? Don't you dare.

Blinking hard, Laney braced her palms on the kitchen counter. At the moment she didn't care what Beckett had to say, or Jude, or anyone else on the planet. Her only desire was to get through the door, scurry out back to the cottage she'd shared with Beckett for five precious weeks and lock the world away. That plan was squashed when she saw that the tables hadn't been wiped down after the lunch service. With a sigh, she tied an apron loosely around her waist and headed for the dining room with a rag. She began her work, ignoring Beckett, who was standing near the wide side windows that looked out toward the hot springs. That reminded her of another thing she had to do before she could call it a night: lock the gates that led to the spring to discourage trespassers. There was never a single moment when the to-do list was finished, and most of the time she didn't mind. Right now, every limb screamed for a nap. She'd whisked two tabletops clean before Beckett found his voice.

"Can you...? I mean...will you sit with me? For a minute?"

She knew him well enough to realize he would not leave until he'd said his piece. Best to get it over with. Her slight nod must have been enough encouragement because he went to "their" table, the old rickety round one in the corner next to a spindly ficus. Nicks and dents marred the surface, but it was the spot where so many precious conversations had taken place, where their friendship had morphed into a love that would last, or so she'd thought.

The ancient rotary phone on the wall rang. It had been such a long time since anyone called the old thing. Most people went through their website for information and booking.

"Hotsprings Hotel," she said, feigning a cheerfulness she did not feel. There was no reply. "Hello? Is anyone there?"

There was still no answer, but she thought she caught the faintest sound of a presence on the other end of the line. When no one spoke, she hung up.

"Who was that?" Beckett said, standing while she joined him at the table.

"Wrong number, I guess. No one was there."

His brow furrowed as she took a seat opposite him and hoisted Admiral onto her lap. The dog sported his fall bandanna, decorated with pumpkins. "You are a handsome doggy," she told him as she stroked his head.

"He looks like he's doing well."

She kept her eyes on the dog. "His heart isn't strong, Doc Parson says, but I take good care of him."

"I don't doubt that for a second. I remember you staying up with him all night long when he got the doggy flu."

She kissed Admiral and fondled his ears. Beckett watched her, silent until she could stand it no longer. "What do you need to tell me?"

He darted a look around, but there were no patrons occupying the space.

Admiral looked up as Jude entered.

Laney beckoned him over, and he pulled up a chair.

"Snake's been removed. Animal control will release it in the canyon."

"Thank you. Beckett was just going to tell me why he's here. You might as well hear it too."

Beckett flashed Jude an irritated look. He had probably hoped for a few moments alone with her, but it was the opposite of what she wanted. The only way around Beckett's determination was to hear him out and send him on his way. Unless he'd decided to keep sole ownership of the hotel after all. The prickle of panic fluttered her nerves.

If that happened, she'd find another way to support herself. She'd never been afraid of hard work.

Beckett cleared his throat. "Pauline Sanderson's brother Kenny had his buddies deliver a message to me in jail."

Jude arched an eyebrow. "That why your face is busted up?"

"Yeah." He sucked in a breath and let it out. "He's threatened to kill me for what he thinks I did to his sister."

Her mouth fell open. "He arranged to have you beaten up in jail? He got away with that?"

"That's not the point. If he comes after me, I'll handle it." He shifted. "He's threatened to kill you too, Laney."

Her stomach flip-flopped. "And that's why you came back? To tell me?"

He nodded.

She didn't know what she'd expected

him to say, but that wasn't it. The murder, his jail time and all that had happened since then, the divorce papers and now some other threat. All of a sudden, she was desperate to get away from it all. "All right. Thank you for letting me know. I need to go lie down." She rose.

"You don't understand," he blurted, reaching for her hand. His fingers were warm and calloused, but his touch felt strange, as if her skin did not recognize the feel of him anymore. "It's serious. This guy is dangerous. The snake, the phone-call hang up... It could be him. You have to listen to me."

"No, I don't." She hated the quiver in her own voice. "I listened to you once."

His gaze flickered. "Please," he said, low and soft.

Now her stomach was in full-on rebellion. She breathed through her nose, fighting for calm. To her dismay, Jude gestured for her to stay. Cradling Admiral, she once more perched uneasily in the chair.

"Kenny Sanderson is a bad dude, no

question. We looked at him as a possible suspect after Pauline was murdered," Jude said.

Beckett cocked his head. "Thought you closed the case when you decided I'd done it."

Jude ignored the gibe. "Like I said, we investigated. Kenny was out on parole for assault at the time Pauline was killed, and he was wearing an ankle bracelet, so he had an alibi. They apparently had a close relationship, so we concluded we were barking up the wrong tree. And, of course, we had a suspect with Pauline's bloody sweater in his car."

Beckett's mouth was bracketed by deep lines. He looked more exhausted than she was. "Do you know where Kenny is now?"

Jude got up. "I'll make a phone call. Be right back."

Laney did not want to sit at the table with Beckett staring at her, so she excused herself to the kitchen and drank some water. Patting her neck with a moistened towel restored her somewhat. Beckett had to be wrong about Kenny Sanderson targeting her. She'd had nothing to do with his sister's murder. She saw on her cell phone that she'd missed a call. That would just have to wait until she'd managed to convince Beckett to leave.

When Jude returned to the table, she rejoined them.

"Kenny's in Beatty," Jude said, grimly.

Her breath caught. The tiny town of Beatty was settled, like Furnace Falls, on the Nevada side of Death Valley. "That's only twenty minutes from here."

"I don't want you to worry. He's been checking in with his parole officer as directed, hasn't missed an appointment." Jude studied Beckett for a moment. "There's no proof that he orchestrated your prison attack."

Beckett rubbed his forehead. "I didn't make this all up."

"Are you sure?"

Beckett and Jude stared at each other.

"What are you really doing here, Beck?" Jude said finally.

"What do you mean? I just told you."

"Showing up now, pretending you need to protect Laney. Why?"

A vein jumped in his jaw. "Not pretending anything. She's in danger."

"Is that something you're telling yourself so you can justify coming back to Furnace Falls?"

"No." He slapped both palms on the tabletop. "I'm not making it up. I wouldn't do that."

Jude's expression hardened. "You're not going to get your home back. This town believes you killed Pauline Sanderson, and that's never going to change, so if this is a ploy…"

"Is that what you think, Jude?" Admiral looked up at Beckett's harsh tone, and Laney rubbed the dog's ears to soothe him as Beckett continued. "We're cousins. Our dads grew up together and so did we. You know me. We went all the way from first grade through high school together."

"I *knew* you. You were competitive, wanted to win at any cost."

"What high school boy doesn't want to win?"

"Yeah, but you wanted it so much that you almost killed Dan. He was a good guy. He's still a good guy, in spite of what you did to him. He's made a life for himself without his vision."

Laney wanted to cover her ears. The pain that had rippled out from that decades-old accident had shipwrecked not only Dan's life but Beckett's too. "Jude..."

Jude ignored her. "My job is to keep order in this town and to help Laney when I can since you left her high and dry."

Beckett jerked to his feet, earning a startled yip from Admiral. "All right. You'll never believe me that I'm innocent. I understand that. But this isn't about me anymore. It's not a ploy—it's real. Kenny is going to come here to hurt her."

Jude crossed his arms. "I will look into it."

Beckett let out a grunt. "Will you? Why doesn't that comfort me?"

Jude leveled a stare at Beckett. "I'll look into it because I'm a cop, and if there is a threat, Laney deserves protection, but it shouldn't come from you. You've done enough. Get on out of here, Beckett. This isn't your home anymore."

Now she really did feel the burn of tears behind her lids. Not his home. She wasn't sure it was hers anymore either. Would there ever be a person she'd want to make a home with? Could she ever stake everything on another man who pledged faithfulness in sickness and in health? She caught her lip between her teeth and closed her eyes against the sudden dizziness.

Beckett tensed. "What's wrong, Laney? Are you sick?"

"I'm fine."

"You're so pale..." Beckett started.

"I said I'm fine." She hurried off. It took every ounce of her strength to push her way across the floor. She had to keep going. There was no other choice. Snuggling Admiral under her chin, she rushed out of the dining room before either man could say another word.

THREE

Beckett wasn't sure what to do with himself, but he was certain as the sunrise that he couldn't leave until he was reasonably confident Kenny or any of his henchmen weren't in the vicinity. Plus, he had another nagging concern that Laney was not in good health. She was the kind of person who never admitted when she was feeling poorly anyway. He recalled her completing a double shift at the hotel before she had consented to seeing a doctor for an undisclosed ailment, which turned out to be an appendix about to rupture.

She'd disappeared somewhere, and he couldn't very well do a room-to-room search.

He figured he might as well make himself useful while he waited for her to re-emerge, so he repaired a broken shutter in the recreation room and a couple of missing shingles to the roof. In spite of the heat baking down on him, he surveyed the property from his bird's-eye view. The camping area, a flat acreage with trailer hookups and platform tents, was nearly deserted. The swimming pool and cabana area was empty, as was the horseshoe pit. There were only one or two cars in the front lot, indicating a mere handful of guests were staying in the main house. Fall was usually gearing up for prime visitor time. Not now.

Perhaps the new resort, complete with all the modern trimmings, that had opened up fifteen miles away was luring away customers. His gut told him the real reason. A murdered woman on the property, the owner jailed for the crime? Not exactly the ideal ambience for a family vacation. His release was now public knowledge, which would further dissuade patrons. If the hotel failed, what would Laney live on? Fifteen acres of sun-blasted ground unsuitable for pretty much anything? He climbed down from the roof, steeped in new worry. The hotel was all he had to give to Laney, and it had to survive to support her.

Wiping the sweat from under the brim of his old fire-department baseball cap, he put his tools back in the shed and strolled past the empty picnic tables that hugged the late-afternoon shade. Sooner or later Laney would have to show up for the dinner service. He made sure to keep an eye out, popping into the kitchen to lend a hand. Herm was there like he'd been since shortly after Beckett's father took ownership. He glanced up from filling a hefty platter with sliced brisket.

"Beckett," he said. His grin revealed one missing front tooth, which he told everyone was from a Vietnam War injury but Beckett knew was the result of slipping on a sandy sidewalk. "Good to see you." He clasped Beckett in a wiry hug before he went back to his slotted spoon.

"Thanks, Herm." He inhaled a deep lungful of the garlic mashed potatoes and succulent meat. "That smells fantastic."

"Oughta be—I've been perfecting the recipe for a couple of decades. Here, let me dish you up a plate. You look like you haven't eaten since the eighth grade."

"Put me aside some, okay? I'm looking for Laney. Worried about her."

Herm became suddenly busy wiping down his workspace.

"Herm?"

"Yeah?" No eye contact.

"Do you know something about Laney? About her health maybe? She looks tired and stressed."

"Naw. Imagine it's a shock, you being back and all. Poor lady's been through it, you know?" Still he continued to wipe the already clean counter.

"Has she been sick?"

"Don't think so. Say, I got to get this food in the warming oven and start on the potatoes."

It was clear Herm wasn't going to betray any private information about Laney, and though his instincts were prickling, he respected Herm for doing his best for her. "All right. One more question. There's someone staying on the property, a lady with a dark braid. Know anything about her?"

"Name's Rita something." He whacked the slotted spoon against the side of the pot to shake off the juices. "Brown. Rita Brown. Checked in two days ago."

Two days ago. Right after Beckett's jail-cell beating. "Alone?"

"Far as I can tell. Since the place is pretty empty, we upgraded her to a nicer room. Seems to stick around the lodge a lot. Haven't heard of her going into the park yet. Why would someone come and stay here without going to see the sights? Odd."

Odd, for sure. The muscles deep in the pit of his stomach tightened. "Thanks, Herm." The cook saluted as he left the kitchen.

He heard the high tone of a female voice

coming from the back porch. He found Laney there sitting on a wooden swing talking on her cell phone. "Thank you for calling, Irene. I'll do my best."

She must be talking to the local doctor, Irene Kincaid. Irene and Laney had been fast friends since Irene had opened up her practice in Furnace Falls five years prior. So was Laney sick? He realized she'd disconnected and now she was crying. That paralyzed him. Barge in or retreat? The last thing he wanted to do was upset her further or pry into her personal life.

He knew in his bones he was the reason for her sadness, and he feared distressing her more. While he attempted to ease backward, Admiral poked his head up from Laney's lap and offered a happy whine and tail wag at him.

Laney looked over.

"I, uh… I'm sorry," he said. "I didn't mean to disturb you." She looked alarmingly exhausted, her eyes shadowed underneath.

She stood, Admiral tucked against her chest. "I have to go help serve dinner."

"I will too."

"No, Beckett. You heard what Jude said. You should go."

"Please listen to me. Kenny is coming here. I'm not leaving you unprotected."

"Leaving me unprotected?" A flash of anger lit the depths of her eyes. "You didn't worry about that when you filed for divorce."

Pain cut through him like a buzz saw. "I did it for you."

She huffed out a breath. "Right. So now that you're out of jail, what happens? You're dropping the divorce proceedings?"

A challenge rang in her tone and his heart sank to his knees. "No," he said. "I'll always be seen as a killer. Divorce will protect you from that. You can take your old name, have a fresh start."

She laughed, a harsh, bitter sound. "Thanks for filling me in on what I should do. It sounds like you've got it all figured out."

She tried to move by him, but he stopped her with an arm on her shoulder. She stiffened under his touch.

"It isn't how I wanted it to turn out," he said, fighting through the lump in his throat. "What else was I supposed to do?"

She didn't look at him, but he heard her convulsive swallow. "You were supposed to love me for better or for worse, like I was prepared to do for you. You broke your vow, Beckett, the promise you made to me on our wedding day."

His throat tightened and he struggled to breathe. "I'm sorry."

She shook her head. "Doesn't matter now. What's gone is gone."

He slowly dropped his hand. Whatever love she'd had for him had evaporated, leaving only the dregs of bitterness behind. What had he expected? He deserved nothing more. She'd been let down time and time again in her life, but nonetheless, she'd put her trust in him and he'd broken it. "I'm sorry," he said again. "You didn't deserve to be treated like that."

She eased away from his grip. "Don't be sorry. Just move on and restart your life. I'll do the same as soon as we sign the papers."

He let her ease away a few steps before he spoke again. "Like I said, I'm sorry, but I'm going to sleep in one of the tents until I'm convinced things are secure here. I'll try to stay out of your way, and I'll make sure the hotel is legally signed over to you before I leave."

Now she turned, and there was an indecipherable expression on her face.

"How long will all that take?"

"I don't know. I won't stay any longer than I need to."

Light shimmered in her blue eyes. "Promise me one thing."

He waited.

Her silence spread out until he shifted uncomfortably.

After another moment more she seemed to come to a decision. "Okay," she said quietly, shoulders squared. "Promise me that you'll leave here and not come back, no matter what you find out."

He frowned. "I don't understand."

"Just promise. After you go, you won't be involved in my life for any reason." She was fighting some strong emotion. "Promise."

"All right," he said. "If that will make you feel better."

Laney hesitated for a moment, then reached into the pocket of her jeans and fished out a bottle. "Irene's call wasn't purely a social one."

His gut cinched. She was sick. He'd guessed right. "Tell me what's wrong."

"Nothing. She wanted to be sure I was taking these."

He looked down at the white bottle, and two words blazed at him like the tiki torches Laney insisted on.

Prenatal vitamins. He read it over and over. "Prenatal..." His gaze flew to her face. "But I thought..."

"So did I," she said, tears beginning to spill from her eyes.

"You're…you're pregnant?"

She nodded. A sad smile curved her trembling lips.

"But I didn't think… I mean…" He gulped. "The doctors said…"

"They were wrong."

He stood there, stunned and silent.

Her voice dropped to barely above a whisper. "Isn't it incredible that God gave us a baby, just as you ended our marriage?"

He couldn't form a thought. Laney was pregnant with their child.

"Laney…"

She shook her head, lips pressed tight together. "This doesn't change anything, Beckett. Remember your promise. You're leaving, and you're not coming back," she said before she disappeared into the kitchen.

As she plastered on a smile, passing out the platters of meat and potatoes to the

handful of diners, Laney's insides quivered at what she'd revealed. She hadn't
wanted to tell him, but she knew he'd find
out. Worse than having him stick around
out of some sort of need to protect her
would be him lingering out of guilt.

He'd promised to leave, and he believed
it better than tainting her with his reputation. Would he feel the same now that he
knew she was carrying their child?

"Doesn't matter," she muttered savagely.
"He won't be your husband anymore in a
few weeks." A baby, even from a woman
who wasn't supposed to be able to conceive, wouldn't change that.

"Snake."

The word cut through her reverie. She
blinked at the woman, taking a few seconds to remember her name. Rita Brown.

"I'm sorry. I was thinking about something else. What did you say?"

The woman lifted a shoulder. "I heard
there was a rattlesnake in your van."

"Yes," Laney said, wondering how that
bit of news had gotten around. "Probably

crawled into the camping supplies. The perils of living in a desert."

"There are a lot of perils here," Rita said, running a finger around the edge of her water glass.

Laney tried for another smile. "Well, it is one of the hottest places in the world. The record is one hundred thirty-five degrees Fahrenheit. They don't call it Death Valley for nothing."

"And you had a murder on the property four months ago."

Laney stared. "It's not something we talk about."

Rita's intense gaze did not waver. "I heard your husband was out of jail. They mishandled some evidence or something. Word around town is people think he's guilty." She cocked her head. "But you don't think so, do you?"

Now the hairs on the back of Laney's neck stood up. She lifted her chin. "Can I get you some dessert?" she said stiffly. "Our cook has made a delicious apple cobbler."

"No, thanks," Rita said, standing. "I'm not here for the food."

Rita wasn't there for the food, nor did she show any particular interest in the area.

So why exactly was she there?

The wall phone rang, and Laney jumped. It rang again and she stared at the old clunky thing. Calls were few and far between, and now two in one day.

Rita's mouth twisted into a grin. "Shouldn't you answer that?" she said over her shoulder as she left the dining room.

Laney picked it up, her gaze still following Rita's departure. "Hotsprings Hotel."

There was a long pause. "Is this the property owned by Beckett Duke?" It was a man's voice.

Her pulse ticked up. "Who is calling, please?"

Silence.

"Who is this?"

The caller abruptly disconnected. Laney found that her hand shook as she hung up the phone. She called Jude on her cell and reported the strange incident. He promised to check the phone records to see where the call had originated.

Rita's prying and the call plagued Laney through the dinner service, or maybe it was Beckett's agitated presence. It was all she could do to keep away from him, clearing dishes, helping arrange a tour of the national park the following day, preparing the coffeepot for the morning breakfast service. Should she tell him about the call? But the police were investigating, and surely there was no reason to discuss anything with Beckett. The farther she could stay away from him, the better.

At last she saw him stride off toward his tent, and she figured she might have gotten free of him at least for the evening. She knew he probably wanted to discuss the baby, but as far as she was concerned, there was nothing more to talk about. The papers were ready to go to the lawyer; she'd see to that when she had a spare moment. Perhaps she could convince Jude to discuss security plans or some such thing with Beckett and then he'd be cleared to leave, this time for good.

The sun set into a molten swirl of color, and with it went her remaining energy. Admiral's waggling behind reminded her there was one chore left: secure the gate to the hot springs.

"All right, Admiral," she said, taking the key ring from the peg by the back kitchen door. "Shall we finish up and call it a night?" She had a new chapter of a travelogue to read and a baggie of vanilla wafers waiting for her, not to mention a nice bacon-flavored chewy treat for Admiral. The old dog waddled along and she kept her pace slow so he would not get left behind or overexert himself.

As she trudged, she let the whisper of cool autumn air revive her. The scenery never failed to lift her spirits as she surveyed the glorious sprawl of the Inyo Mountains in the distance. The vast desert soothed her, as it had since she'd come to live here with Kitty Duke, Jude's mother. Kitty found her hungry and hopeless, in a Las Vegas bus stop, took her in and found her work at the Hotsprings. Aunt Kitty, as Laney called her, was the mother she was meant to have.

"God saved you then," she murmured to the night sky, "and He'll watch over you and your baby now too."

Inhaling deeply of the scent of the desert at night, she started off. She climbed the sloping trail until she got to the spot where the spring lay caged in on one side by trees, the mountains poking out above. The mineral-rich water steamed as the air cooled around the oblong patch of milky water that hovered between ninety-five and one hundred and seven degrees, depending on the season. It was a perennial favorite of the guests. The springs were a jewel unique to the Hotsprings Hotel, a brilliant gem in a dull, sandy setting. A jet roared over, a common occurrence since the military used the valley for their flight exercises. Her good friend Willow, another of Beckett's cousins, was currently dating a pilot training there.

She made her way along the gravel path to the arm of the gate, using her key to unfasten the padlock threaded through a metal loop. As she tugged on the arm to pull it across the access, something rustled in the shrubs.

A wild burro, probably. One of the many that frequented the area. Usually they were not a problem until visitors mistook them for the tamer variety and tried to get too close. The bossy, ornery critters were anything but docile.

Admiral cocked an ear. She paused. Had he heard something? Nerves tingled along her spine.

After a moment, he continued nosing around in hopes of finding small bits of dropped snacks.

Feeling foolish, she began to pull the gate closed. It fought her as it always did, the metal squealing in defiance.

Admiral barked at the sound, the hair standing up on his neck.

"It's okay, sweetie. I'll get some oil on it as soon as I can."

There was nothing to alarm her until a stirring of air caused her to look up, just as a rock came hurtling toward her temple.

FOUR

A baby.

Beckett stood in the middle of the musty canvas tent. Though the surroundings were familiar, the wood frames housing two twin mattresses, a small set of drawers, the plain lamp and footlocker containing extra blankets and a Bible, he felt like he had landed on another planet.

Even locked up in jail like a rabid animal, he had not felt anywhere near this level of bewilderment.

Laney was pregnant…in spite of the doctor's dire proclamation after her failed pregnancy when she was a teen. Something about her uterus. They'd intended someday to adopt, but never in their wildest dreams did they expect to have a biological child. He experienced alternating waves of elation and anguish.

A little life was silently growing inside Laney, cocooned and secret. He wanted to scoop his wife up and hold her, to somehow be close to the incredible phenomenon taking place.

His wife, their child... Reality rushed back in a wash of bitterness.

Why now, would God grant their deepest desire? When their marriage was over? Their future in tatters? He remembered the woman from town who'd seen him being led to the squad car after his arrest.

"You deserve to rot in jail," she'd spit.

Did he deserve this too? To lose everything?

There is no condemnation for those who follow Jesus, Miss Kitty used to say when he'd begun to visit regularly as an excuse to see Laney outside their hotel duties. Miss Kitty had seen her own share of trouble, including abandonment by her abusive husband, but she clung to the Lord with the unflagging strength of a cactus holding tight to a desert cliff. Why couldn't he do that? Perhaps because deep down he didn't believe he was worthy of that kind of great love. No condemnation? That wasn't the life he knew.

His mind returned to the baby. When would it be born? Would it be a son or daughter? The thoughts both tortured and tantalized him.

He was in such a fog he didn't at first hear the high-pitched yip followed by a wheeze.

Admiral plowed into the tent. The dog's tongue hung out in a fleshy pink ribbon and he was wheezing, eyes bulging more than usual. Beckett dropped to his knees. Admiral collapsed and let out a pitiful whine. He'd obviously been running, but Admiral was never out of Laney's sight and she was nowhere to be seen.

A fist of fear punched Beckett in the gut.

He scooped up the exhausted dog and ran out of the tent. Lights burned in the main house. Herm would be in the kitchen cleaning up before heading to his own cramped room on the property. He would have heard Laney if she called for help, or found the agitated dog and come running.

He stumbled to a halt, his eyes drifting to the trail that stretched away toward the springs. He jerked a look at his watch, a gift from Laney on their wedding day. Seven forty. She would have gone to lock the gate to secure the hot spring. Holding Admiral like a football, he sprinted. His heart thundered in time to his panicked thoughts. He'd left her alone. Kenny had found her.

The gravel slipped under his steel-toed boots, but he held firmly to Admiral and did not slacken his pace. Panic like he had never known filled him to bursting.

"Laney," he shouted when he was within a hundred yards. There was no answer. The gate was unlocked, the metal arm pulled only partially across the opening. "Laney," he yelled again.

He shoved through the gate.

Lord, he prayed, *please.* His shipwrecked

life was not redeemable and he did not ask the Lord for any favors, but Laney... Laney did not deserve an ounce more pain...and the baby... That innocent life should not pay for the mistakes of his or her father. The setting sun glinted off the water, setting the surface aglow. "Where are you?" he hollered again.

"Here."

He thought at first he'd imagined it. Stopping quickly, he almost lost his balance. The wind tickled the leaves in the shrubbery. There was no sign of an intruder, nor Laney. Admiral yipped.

"I'm here." Laney's voice came again, but he still could not figure out from where. He eased Admiral down.

"Where is she, buddy?"

Admiral had recovered enough to heave himself along the rough ground and around the spring, toward a pile of boulders.

Beckett scrambled after him, trying to avoid getting his boots stuck between the rocks. Admiral whined.

Behind the pile of granite he found her. Her hair framed blue eyes wide with fear. She sat huddled in a ball, arms around her knees. Admiral scrambled next to her, and she scooped him up. Beckett forced some level of calm into his voice, though his insides were jumping like frogs at sundown as he crouched next to her.

"What happened? Are you hurt? Did you fall? Are you bleeding?"

She pressed her lips together and cocked an eyebrow. "Which question do you want me to answer first?"

Sass. That was good. "Let's start with are you hurt?"

She considered. "Not really, but my foot is stuck between two rocks." Though she was all calm and bravado on the surface, her face was pale. She pressed the dog close.

Beckett bent to look. "Tell me what happened while I get you out of here."

She hesitated a moment. "I was coming up to lock the gate. I felt someone was behind me. When I turned to look, this rock came sailing out of nowhere." She swallowed. "If I hadn't ducked, it would have clobbered me."

He made an effort to unclench his jaw. "Did you see who threw it?"

"No. Whoever it was hid in the bushes. I ran behind the rocks, but my foot got wedged and I dropped my cell phone. I heard someone running away. I was going to make sure they were gone before I started yelling for help. Then Admiral took off. I thought he was scared. I didn't know my doggy hero was going to send for reinforcements." She turned her face away from him and rested it on Admiral's back, as if she didn't want to look at him. He heard a sniff that struck him to the core. She was fighting tears.

With the lightest of touches, he placed a palm on the crown of her head. "It's okay. You did the right thing to try to hide." Still she did not look at him, so he pulled his hand away and finished separating the rocks to free her. Taking her elbow before she could refuse the help, he raised her to a standing position.

"How does your ankle feel?"

She put weight on it. "Okay. Just scraped, I think."

He held her hand while they eased away from the rock pile. "I need to find my cell phone," she said.

"I'll come back at first light and get it."

When they reached the side of the pool, he noticed that her legs were trembling and there was blood on her sock. In one fluid movement, he lifted her up, Admiral still in her arms.

She stiffened. "I don't need you to carry me."

He didn't answer, just made his way along the path. Her head was tucked under his chin. She'd always been a perfect fit. He was all bristly stubbornness and hardheaded determination, and Laney was the only one in the world who could see past that into the soul of him. He swallowed. It was exquisite pain to hold her, to know the love they'd shared was only alive in his memory.

She squirmed. "You're being silly. I can walk."

"You're pregnant."

"I'm quite aware of that."

"I'll put you down when we get back to the lodge."

She heaved a sigh but did not reply. It seemed as though she weighed nothing at all. Was she eating enough? Was the baby growing properly?

"Too tight," she said.

He realized he was clasping her to his chest too snugly and he eased up. "Sorry." He also slowed his pace a fraction to prevent jostling her. Not too much, as he considered the fact that the rock thrower may not have actually left the property. He could still be here, with dozens of places to hide.

When they reached the house, he elbowed the kitchen door open and settled her into a chair.

Herm entered, holding a stack of coffee mugs, face etched with alarm.

"I'm okay," Laney said before he could speak.

"Call the police," Beckett said. "She was attacked."

"Actually…" Laney started, but Herm was already off-loading his burden and heading for the phone. Beckett fetched a first-aid kit and peeled off her shoe and sock.

"I'll call Dr. Irene soon as I clean this up," Beckett said.

"I don't need her."

He dabbed at her ankle with a disinfectant wipe. "Sorry if it stings. Dr. Irene might need to check the baby. Make sure your blood pressure's okay and stuff."

"I'm perfectly fine."

He still didn't look at her. "Or do an ultrasound, to check for…"

Laney took his chin and tipped it up so he was staring into her pale blue eyes. He went still.

"Beckett," she said calmly. "I do not

need to see a doctor. I am fine. The baby is fine. A scraped ankle does not require an exam."

He was suspended there for a moment, immobilized by her touch, stopped by the weight of what he'd lost. "I... Okay."

She folded forward in the chair and watched as he applied a bandage to the scrape on her ankle. "Admiral needs water."

"Got it," Herm said, filling a shallow bowl for the dog, who lapped it with sloppy enthusiasm. "Jude is on his way."

"Thanks, Herm." Beckett noted the carafes of coffee and hot water on the counter. "I figured you'd have the kitchen packed up by now. Someone checking in after hours?" he said hopefully.

"No, sadly. Got a guest returning late for the night. Waiting to see if she wanted anything 'fore I got the kitchen buttoned up."

A guest out late? "What guest?"

"Rita Brown. Said she was going out on a starlight photography tour."

"Yeah? Cloudy for stargazing." Wrong time of year too. The dazzling display of stars unaffected by light pollution was most vivid in winter and spring, earning Death Valley the designation as the largest Dark Sky National Park in the country.

Herm shrugged. "Only have so many vacation days, I guess," he said. "Maybe she couldn't wait for clearer skies."

The best photography outfit around happened to be run by his cousin Willow Duke. If Rita Brown had really been on a photography tour, he'd find out soon enough from Willow. If Rita was caught in a lie, well, perhaps then maybe she'd had something to do with the rock tossed at Laney.

Either way, he was going to find out exactly who was responsible.

Laney laid the facts out for Jude in as thorough a manner as she could in between Beckett's interjections. Now Admiral was back in her lap, snoring away. Her ankle did not hurt much. Knowing someone had thrown a rock at her head disturbed her far more.

Was Beckett correct and this Kenny Sanderson really was after her? Or had it just been mischievous kids with nothing to do but stir up trouble? There were two teen boys staying at the hotel, plus dozens of bored young adults in the town of Furnace Falls. Small desert town, not much in the way of entertainment. They'd had minor problems before with vandalism and trespassers sneaking into the hot springs.

"I'll talk to the kids on the property," Jude said.

"It's not teens." Beckett folded his arms.

"I already know what your theory is." Jude frowned. "I've got a call in to Kenny's parole officer to confirm his whereabouts. He's staying at his uncle's trailer. Right now Kenny's not at home, but it's still well within his parole curfew hours and his schedule is cleared with his PO so he can work at the gas station until ten p.m. I also have a cop staged outside the uncle's trailer to see when exactly he does show up and ask him a few questions."

"Can you call his cell phone?" Beckett asked.

"His parole officer did at my request. Kenny's not answering, but that's to be expected. Boss at the gas station forbids them from having a phone on them during work hours."

Beckett did not look mollified, but at least he didn't antagonize Jude further. "And the guest? The one who's out late?"

"Rita Brown," Laney said.

Jude raised an eyebrow. "How is she a part of this?"

Beckett frowned. "I don't know, but there's just something odd about her."

"That sounds about right for someone in Furnace Falls. Odd doesn't give me grounds to interrogate her."

"Then I will."

He frowned. "No, you won't."

They were nose to nose, both big framed and square chinned, as were most of the Duke men. Stubborn was another trait they shared equally. Laney stood up, drawing their attention. "I'm with Jude on this one, Beckett. Rita is not the norm, but we can't afford to alienate visitors with a nearly empty hotel on our hands. We need every guest we can get at this point."

"I wasn't able to trace the call to the hotel you told me about," Jude said.

She nodded and rolled her ankle to test the bandage.

"Do you need me to...?" Beckett started.

"I am perfectly fine to walk to my room and tuck myself in."

"At least let me carry the dog."

Before she could argue, Beckett had taken the solid lump from her. Though she wouldn't admit it, it was easier not to tote his dead weight along. Beckett followed her down the hallway and across the sprawling courtyard to their cabin. She opened the door and turned to take Admiral from him, but he was already moving past her. After setting the dog down, he began checking the windows and the door, which opened onto a minuscule porch area that housed her collection of desert plants. Aghast, she watched him take a quick glance into the closet and under the bed.

He fixed her with a scowl. "You need to keep everything locked."

She stared at him, refusing to be bossed. "Thank you for the advice. I've learned how to take care of myself."

His mouth tightened. "I mean it."

"Beckett, what happened might have just been teens out for excitement. Let's not blow this all out of proportion."

"It's not teens."

"You don't know that."

"Laney," he said, eyes ablaze with emotion that kicked up her nerves. "I did not kill Pauline Sanderson."

It was not what she had expected him to say. "I know."

He exhaled, long and slow. "I'm glad you still believe me about that, anyway."

She looked down. "I never doubted it. I told you as much, even at the jail before you stopped letting me visit."

He blinked hard, and she saw his Adam's apple move. It took a few minutes for him to be able to speak. "Pauline's murderer was never caught."

Never caught.

His expression went distant, as if he were peering at something a thousand miles away. "I've had a lot of time to think it over. They set me up from the beginning, leaving a note for me to meet Pauline, putting her sweater in my truck. It was premeditated."

A prickle of gooseflesh erupted across her shoulders. She didn't want to think about that terrible night, but she could not walk away from the conversation.

He continued. "There was no apparent motive for the crime. She still had money in her pocket. There was another reason someone wanted her dead."

Laney felt the thud of her heart whacking against her ribs. In spite of her fear, she made herself ask. "What are you saying?"

"Even if you don't believe Kenny is a threat, there's still a killer at large."

"That would be foolish in a small town like this. I'm sure they're long gone by now, someone traveling through, a stranger."

"Maybe or maybe not. There's a possibility it's someone who stayed right here, someone we know and trust, who needed to silence Pauline for some reason."

Someone we know and trust. "I'll keep the door locked, I promise."

"And don't go anywhere alone."

"I'll do what I can, but I've got a hotel to run."

"*We* have a hotel to run, Laney."

She went stock-still. "You're not staying."

"Not permanently, but I'm here until you're safe. I told you and I wasn't kidding."

She glared. "I don't want you shadowing me like some sort of bodyguard."

His lips quirked with the hint of a smile. "I'll be subtle…like a bull in a china shop."

It was their joke from years before when he had dropped an entire tray of dishware in the middle of a dinner service and broken every single piece. Beckett had always said he was not built for interior spaces. He proved it by breaking things with regularity until she'd put her collection of porcelain animals up on a high shelf. She would not allow herself to be caught up in nostalgia.

"I don't want you here, but what I want isn't going to change your mind, is it?"

She saw him struggling to compose an answer.

"Nope," he finally said. "Sorry."

She heaved a sigh that felt like it came all the way from her toes. "All right, but remember, Beckett, this is temporary. We are getting a divorce. When Kenny is captured, one of us is leaving this hotel."

"It's going to be deeded to you, just like I said, Laney."

"You don't have to do that. You're out of jail now. You can run it, and I'll go."

"It's yours and..." He took a breath. "Yours and the baby's."

The way he said it made her eyes pool,

but she would not let them spill. Silently, she nodded.

"Is it...? I mean...do you know if it's a girl or boy?"

Pain circled through her in burning waves. Somehow, she got the words out. "I don't know. Aunt Kitty thinks it's a girl."

For a moment, his smile stripped the weariness from his face, and the wonder of their child danced between them. "A girl." His gaze roamed her face hungrily. "She'll be every bit as amazing as her mother."

His comment struck her as almost cruel. Amazing? The woman he'd decided to divorce? Before she could reply, Beckett was striding away, shoulders hunched, a long, tall silhouette against the setting sun.

FIVE

Beckett didn't return to the tent. After he retrieved Laney's phone from between some rocks near the spring, he settled in at the battered table in the dining room where he had a clear view of the front parking lot. Rita Brown would return eventually. She'd have to enter through the front or take the long route around to her room, but either way, he'd spot her.

He shifted to ease the ache in his battered ribs. The dining room was finally starting to cool as the heat of the day dissipated. His view out the front window pained him. Though the wide vista of multihued rock was gorgeous, it reminded him of what he'd held most dear and lost. A swirl of tiny shadows danced along the horizon, bats on their evening forage. The sun finally surrendered and sank fully behind the distant cliffs.

Jude had settled himself in the kitchen to return phone calls. Beckett made use of the time to do some investigation on his own, texting his cousin Willow to check if Rita had been on her starlight tour. Jude would not approve of him making inquiries, but Beckett was past caring.

I'm out with Tony, she texted back. No tour tonight. Too cloudy.

Tony Ortega was the navy pilot Willow had been dating for almost a year. As far as Beckett could tell, the single father was good for his gregarious cousin, who had been hurt too many times in the love department. So...there had been no starlight tour for Rita. Willow was the only one offering organized photography excursions in and around Death Valley, as far as he knew. So where had Rita been? Too cloudy for good photo ops. Nightlife was next to nil in Furnace Falls. Neighboring Beatty, with a population just over one thousand, offered a few restaurants, a historical museum and a handful of small shops, so it was possible she'd taken a quick trip there, but most everything would have been closed hours earlier. The roads were long and isolated, and it would be easy for an out-of-towner to become disoriented. Not smart to go out exploring alone.

Beckett sat quietly, arms folded, the picture of patience. He imagined how his father would laugh looking at him now. As a teen, Beckett had resented working long hours at the hotel. Like most of his peers, he'd wanted to be out riding horses, practicing football, basketball and playing arcade games. Beckett had fancied himself a skilled athlete with a possible professional career. Instead, he'd been required to change linens, take out trash and carry luggage, tasks he'd felt were beneath him. What a fool he'd been.

It pained him to think of his teenage personality, restless and selfish. Life had steamed the impatience out of him. A day spent emptying trash cans and changing bed linens now seemed like what his father used to tell him was *God's work*. After his train wreck of a life, he wasn't sure anything he did would be valued by God. God watched over other people, not Beckett.

Waiting did not bother him at all now, not if it meant he could poke the bushes to shed some light on who'd thrown a rock at Laney. In order to do that, he could be as patient as a stone statue and just as still.

Clouds hemmed in the moonlight so it only shone in patches over the dry ground. In the past they'd keep the front windows open to allow the precious fall cool to seep in, but he'd closed and locked them, the entrance doors, as well. He would take no chances with Laney and the baby's safety. A baby... The realization hit him afresh that there was a little life wrapped snugly inside his wife. *Almost your ex-wife...* He swallowed, his throat suddenly dust dry.

The room was stuffy, but still he sat.

When Rita finally let herself into the

lodge at a few minutes to nine, he was ready. She was moving unhurriedly, carrying no packages or a camera, just a pack big enough for her cell phone and keys.

"Good evening," he said.

She jumped. "Oh, hi. I didn't see you there."

"Sorry I startled you."

"What are you doing sitting all alone?"

He kept his tone neutral. "I like to be sure all the guests are safely returned for the night."

Her eyes gleamed the same dark color as her braid. "That's pretty good service. From what I heard, you had to take a hiatus from your hotel duties."

"I'm back now."

Her sharp gaze roamed his face. "The gossip is they had to free you on a technicality, something about mishandled evidence."

He tensed at her boldness. "I didn't kill her."

She flashed a *Mona Lisa* smile. "Does anyone in this Podunk town believe that?"

He swallowed a flash of anger. "The people that matter believe it. What are you doing here right now? Late to be out, isn't it?"

"Not that it's any of your business, but my night photography plans weren't successful, so I drove around for a while." She lifted a shoulder. "I'm getting some tea before I head to bed."

He wasn't in the mood for coy, not with Laney and the baby in danger. "Why are you here at this hotel? Now? No family, no interest in the park, and you seem to know all about what happened to Pauline."

Her hand went to her hip. "Everyone in town knows what happened, and my reasons for coming to Furnace Falls are my business. Do you always interrogate your guests like this?"

"When my wife gets a rock thrown at her head."

Rita's expression was inscrutable. She showed neither surprise nor guilt. Had she known? Had she been a part of it? "When did that happen?"

He ignored the question. "Are you working for Kenny Sanderson?" he blurted. Bull in a china shop in more ways than one.

Her eyes narrowed. "Who's that?"

There was the smallest something in her voice that didn't ring true. "Pauline Sanderson's brother, but you're so well-informed you know that already, don't you?"

"I may have heard the name." She flipped back her braid. "But I don't work for him. I don't work for anyone in this town. I'm my own boss."

"And what exactly is your line of work?"

She laughed. "I don't have to stand here and get the third degree, especially on my vacation. Good night, Mr. Duke." She strolled to the door, fingering the keys to her room. He wished they'd had enough money to change to the more secure card entry.

After a pause, she looked over her shoulder at him. "For what it's worth, I do believe you're innocent of Pauline's death. So maybe you should treat me better.

Seems like you could use an ally around here."

He twitched. Her tone was sly and calculating. Was she toying with him? Did she have information about what had really happened to Pauline? He got to his feet, wanted to press harder, to force her to come clean, but all he could do was watch her go. Why did she believe him innocent? Because she knew the guilty party?

His blood chilled. Or maybe she was the guilty party?

Exhausted as Laney was, she tossed and turned, twisting the sheets and earning a bleary blink from Admiral, who was curled next to her on the bed. Snatches of nightmares disturbed her mind when she did manage to doze off. Finally, well before sunrise, she heard the sound of hooves striking hard-packed earth. Throwing on clothes, she left Admiral snoring and stepped outside into the blessedly cool air.

Levi Duke, a leaner, ginger-haired version of his cousin Beckett, was on foot guiding two horses across the property. He ducked his head shyly when he saw her, probably hoping she had not noticed him. He still limped a little, a leftover from an accident a few months before. He was fortunate to have survived. While he'd recovered from his injuries, he'd taken over as manager of the stables on the adjoining land and was on the cusp of buying the stables outright with a friend of his. He appreciated being able to cut across the hotel property. Theirs was a mutually beneficial arrangement, as many of the hotel guests enjoyed riding adventures in and around Death Valley during their stay.

Lately, Levi had taken to riding a few of the more difficult horses at night to train them. Besides, she thought, in the wee hours he didn't need to stop and talk to anyone. He was becoming *solitary as an oyster*, as Aunt Kitty would say.

Clearly, he'd meant to pass on by in his taciturn way, but she called out to him quietly, so as not to startle the horses or awaken the precious few guests on the property. "Good morning, Levi."

He stopped and thumbed his cowboy hat back on his head. "Can't sleep?"

"No. I have a terrible craving for lemonade. I could drink a gallon of it right this second."

He quirked a grin that pulled at the healing scar curving from the corner of his upper lip. "That's better than your other craving for peanut butter and olives. I'll stable these horses and fetch you a glass."

"No need. Just walk me to the kitchen, okay?" She felt silly asking, but Beckett would read her the riot act if she took chances of any kind. Thinking of that rock sailing so near her temple made her shiver. If she wasn't pregnant she might have ignored his advice out of stiff-backed pride, but there was another life to consider now besides her own. It wouldn't hurt to exercise some extra caution for a while.

Levi didn't seem to find her request for an escort unusual, which told her Beckett had filled him in already about his concerns.

He led the horses by their reins with one hand and offered his elbow to her. She took it gratefully, since the path was a bit uneven and the sun had not yet risen to illuminate the dips. Siblings Levi, Austin and Willow were a tight-knit clan, as close as the family should be. Jude, their cousin, was as close as a brother. They all accepted her, for the most part, and tried to support her as best they could when their cousin Beckett was arrested. But did all the Duke cousins truly believe, like she did, that Beckett was innocent? She thought they did, with the exception of Jude.

They didn't speak as they walked, both lost in their own thoughts. Levi stayed on the rear porch while she let herself into the kitchen, smack-dab in the middle of a conversation between Jude and Beckett. They both jerked toward her, and she sighed. Bad timing for sure. She should have waited on the lemonade until the coast was clear. Too late to back out.

"Good morning," she said brightly.

"You didn't..." Beckett started.

"No, I didn't. Levi escorted me here. I needed some lemonade."

He blinked and handed over her cell phone. "At five o'clock in the morning?"

She was going to answer, but Jude interrupted. "It's called a craving. Pregnant women get them." The rest of his comment was implied. *If you'd been around, you'd know that.*

Beckett's expression was caught between guilt and wonder. The raw vulnerability there made her look away.

"Oh, I... Right," he said, marching to the fridge.

There was no sense insisting she could do it herself, as he poured her a glass of lemonade from the jug.

She took it and tried not to gulp it down. Beckett alternated staring at her and glaring at Jude. Whatever she'd walked in on didn't seem to be breaking up anytime soon. The awkward quiet became too much for her to stand. She fidgeted with the glass. "Herm will be here soon to start on breakfast. Are you two going to help crack eggs, or is there some other reason why you're taking up space in my kitchen?"

Jude didn't smile at her teasing tone. "I dropped by to tell Beckett that the teens booked here were accounted for last night. They were playing video games at the time someone threw that rock at you. Their parents and the housekeeper both confirmed it."

"Okay. Might have been someone from town, then," she said, halfway through her lemonade.

By his furrowed brow, she could tell Beckett did not agree, but he was clearly focused on a different issue. "Jude was about to tell me about Kenny."

"Yeah." Jude tucked his thumbs into his belt loops. "I'm only sharing this with you so you don't get ideas of butting in."

"Tell me what?"

Jude let out a breath. "Got a report from a coworker at the gas station where Kenny is employed. She said she saw a knife in his backpack."

Beckett's hands fisted. "Parole violation. Can you arrest him?"

"First we'll do a search of the premises," Jude said. "You know, that pesky evidence thing."

"Funny."

"Parole officer's in court today, so we'll handle the search."

Laney felt the lemonade burn in her stomach.

Beckett glowered. "You sent a unit?"

"Yeah. No sign of life at the trailer. Windows are dark. I have a cop standing by, waiting for me. I'm going to check it out right now."

"I'll go with you."

"No. Cop business."

Beckett put his hands on his hips. "I'm going anyway, Jude."

"I'll arrest you for interference."

"Do what you have to do, but I'm going. I'll stay out of the way. I want to see him for myself. All I need is one look at him and I'll know if he was the one who threw the rock."

Jude scoffed. "You can read minds now?"

"No, but he's got a hot temper, from what his buddies said. If he sees me, he won't be able to keep his intentions under wraps. Kenny's a grenade ready to blow. Let me see if I can pull the pin."

"This may turn out to be nothing more than an error. We may have no grounds to arrest him for a parole violation if we don't find that knife."

"Then I want to see that for myself too."

Laney saw the slow burn kindling in Jude, in direct proportion to the cement-like stubbornness rising in Beckett. It was like being dropped in the middle of a spaghetti Western. She could practically hear the tumbleweed blowing.

Beckett broke the silent standoff first. "He had his pals beat me up in prison. They could have killed me, but they didn't. Instead they did something that would hurt worse—they threatened Laney. How do you think that feels?"

He and Jude exchanged a long look and something passed between them. Was it a glimmer of understanding? Jude had loved a woman deeply and lost her. Was he sympathizing? She had no idea. Why were men so stupendously hard to read? As the silence grew, she was not sure if she should finish her lemonade, start cracking eggs or go fetch Levi in case the two men started a wrestling match right there in the kitchen.

There was a tap at the door and Laney hurried to open it. Beckett got there first and looked through the window, opening the door to a startled Dr. Irene.

She wore a jogging suit, her black hair swept into a messy ponytail, glasses perched on her sweaty nose. Her small home was along the same road as the hotel, and Laney gave her carte blanche to snitch a cup of coffee after her regular early-morning run.

"I'm sorry," Laney said. "I haven't got

the coffee going yet. There have been some distractions."

Irene looked from Beckett to Jude to Laney. "I just bumped into Herm a minute ago near the chicken coop and he told me about the rock throwing. Are you okay?" She searched Laney's face. "Please tell me you are not hurt. Herm said you were fine, but I need to hear that from you because men tend to miss details."

Laney smiled. "I am not hurt. Really and truly, but I am glad to see you, especially now. There's too much testosterone filling up this kitchen."

Irene smothered a smile with her hand.

Beckett relaxed a notch. "I'm glad you're here, Doc. The rock didn't hit her, but she's under stress, so maybe her blood pressure needs checking?"

Irene chuckled. "Somehow, Beckett, I think maybe you are adding to that stress."

"Thank you," Laney said. "That's the truth."

He pulled a sheepish look. "Aww, well…

maybe. Can you stay with her until I get back? I have to go with Jude."

"Certainly."

"Not necessary," Laney said at the same moment. "I'm here to help Herm start breakfast just like every day. I don't need a babysitter, and Irene has a medical practice to attend to."

Irene grinned. "Well, Herm is walking slow today, his arthritis, I expect, so how about I help you crack some eggs while you're waiting for him? I can scoot out when he gets here and the meal is under control. My first appointment isn't until ten. You and I need a chance to chat anyway. Is that scenario agreeable to all parties?"

"Perfect," Beckett said. "Thanks."

Jude looked more resigned than pleased as he turned to Beckett. "If Kenny shows, you're not to be involved, understand me, Beck?"

"Yes."

Irene gaped. "Kenny? Isn't that the name of...?"

Beckett nodded. "Pauline's brother. He's made threats against Laney. I think he's behind the rock throwing."

Her eyes rounded in shock. "He's close? I read in the paper that he was paroled before Pauline was murdered, but I didn't imagine he would settle here."

"Like I said, he's promised payback for what he thinks I did to his sister, and he's not the type to shrug off a vow like that."

"But I thought…" She blushed. "Well, I mean, since you were released from jail, I figured the whole thing was over."

Beckett didn't answer. With one final glance at Laney, he followed Jude out.

Irene's face was still suffused with pink. "That was tactless of me."

Laney filled the coffee machine with fresh grounds and added water before she pushed the brew button. "It's okay. You walked into a mess, for sure."

Irene washed her hands and fetched her favorite pink mug from the cupboard where Laney left it for her. "Are you okay? Truly? I can't imagine how it feels to have

Beckett reappear in your life after he'd asked you for a divorce."

Laney watched morosely as the coffee began to drip into the carafe. "I haven't had time to get used to it. He showed up yesterday, out of the blue. First I find a rattlesnake in the van, and then there he is, telling me Kenny is out for revenge. My head is spinning."

Irene put a palm on her shoulder. "And... does he know about the baby?"

Tears pricked her eyes. "Yes, I had to tell him. I guess he has a right to know, but he promised to leave after this threat is dealt with."

"Is that what you want?"

Laney's chin went up. "Absolutely. The bond we had is broken. He's not my husband any longer, except on paper."

Irene hesitated before filling her cup with coffee. "People make mistakes, Laney, terrible mistakes. This could be a second chance for you. Why don't you wrestle with it awhile and see if you change your mind?"

"I won't."

Irene sipped her coffee. "All right. I'm a doctor, not a counselor. The most important thing right now is taking care of you and the baby. Is the Monday checkup time still okay for you?"

Laney nodded. The same terror flooded in before every appointment, the worry that her baby might not make it, like the other tiny life she'd lost. At nineteen, she'd made terrible choices, desperate for love and protection, which had resulted in a pregnancy with a young man who'd dumped her as soon as he found out. Even though she'd been horrified to learn she was expecting, the miscarriage a month later left her with a bone-deep ache to be followed by the blow of discovering a uterine malformation would preclude any future pregnancies. And here she was... pregnant again. Though she would not breathe her fear into words, the surge of terror that she might lose this baby too was ever present.

Irene seemed to read her thoughts. "Everything is right as rain with the pregnancy."

Laney nodded. Right as rain. The tension in her chest eased a bit. "Yes. I've been eating well, hydrating and taking my vitamins, just like my doctor recommends."

Irene smiled. "Well, you do have an amazing doctor, but you have dark circles under your eyes. Expectant mommies need lots of rest."

"Maybe expectant mommies who don't run hotels." Laney shook her head. "Don't start fussing like Beckett."

"Things must be strange for him too." She paused. "When I heard he was back, I thought your situation might change. I figured he could start fresh now that he's been released, and maybe you could too."

The lemonade suddenly turned sickly sweet in Laney's mouth and she set the glass down. Would it ever be over now? With Pauline's killer free and her brother

Kenny out for revenge? She had the disturbing feeling that a monstrous desert storm was about to bear down upon them again.

Over? Not by a long shot.

SIX

Beckett was careful not to crowd the back
of Jude's police vehicle as they headed
east on Highway 374 to Beatty. He kept
the window open, breathing in as deeply
as he could. After being caged like an animal, he didn't suppose he'd ever be able to
get enough of wide-open spaces and clean
desert air, the smell of freedom. He tried
not to remember the raucous jail noises,
the nauseating scent of sweat and indus-
trial cleaner, the taste of cafeteria food he
had to force himself to swallow.

That's behind me now. But was it really? Was there some other enemy waiting
to drop the next bombshell in addition to
Kenny? Again he wondered if he would
always be looking over his shoulder,

waiting for the next explosion. It was not what Laney deserved, not that it mattered. Nothing had changed in that regard. He would forever be seen as a murderer, and he could not trap her in that same net.

He rolled the window farther down, hoping the rush of air would blow away his pain.

Beatty was a small Nevada town, snuggled at the end of Oasis Valley and near the head of the Amargosa River. With a population barely over 1,000, it was still larger than Furnace Falls. Beatty boasted a few shops, a small hotel, trailer parks and a minuscule post office, but it grandly proclaimed itself as the gateway to Death Valley National Park. He could make the drive to Beatty and into the park itself with his eyes closed, having done it countless times to shuttle hotel visitors. That notion pricked at him as he remembered the snake in Laney's van.

A reptilian stowaway? He didn't believe it for a moment. Kenny was behind that stunt. What would have happened to Laney and the baby if she'd been bitten? Jaw clamped tight, he made a mental note as soon as he returned to be sure Laney had no intentions of taking any more groups into the park. He wasn't sure how he would handle that job while keeping a firm eye on Laney, but somehow he'd manage. He wished his cousin Austin was not off on his latest climbing trip, no doubt in one of those places he could only access via his small plane. Austin had always been the first to help and the last to quit.

They rattled through the Boulder Peak Mobile Home Park entrance. The forty trailer units were permanently settled on both sides of the wide dirt streets. Some had rocky landscaping and neatly tended shrubbery. Others sat on bare patches of gravel. Most had sturdy porch structures to provide precious shade. Since it was only just dawn, there were no kids outside playing with the numerous bicycles parked under porch awnings.

One truck rumbled by, the older female

driver waving to Jude in his official car. She shot Beckett a friendly look that immediately turned sour once she determined who he was. He didn't remember ever meeting her, but she obviously knew him, maybe from the papers and newscasts that splashed his picture everywhere after the arrest. He kept his eyes fixed on Jude's bumper. They found the trailer belonging to Leonard Sanderson, Kenny's uncle. Beckett parked across the street and pulled the ball cap down over his brow in case any of the residents were peering from behind their blinds.

"Stay out of the way," Jude cautioned to Beckett. With a hand on his sidearm, he and his officer stationed themselves on either side of the peeling front door.

Jude knocked. "This is the Inyo County police. We need to talk to Kenny Sanderson."

There was no answer. Beckett judged from the cops' rigid postures that they were feeling the same tension he was.

"Police," Jude bellowed. "Open the door."

Beckett got out, nerves taut, but he stayed by his truck, willing his feet to stay put. Jude rapped again at the door, repeating his command. A harrowing three minutes went by and he saw Jude tense as the door creaked open.

A man with greasy brown hair and an unkempt beard looked out. Beckett edged closer so he could hear the conversation.

"Leonard Sanderson?"

"Yeah?"

"I'm Sheriff Jude Duke. Where's your nephew?"

"What's it to you?"

"We're executing a search on behalf of his parole officer."

He threw up his hands. "What now? I don't know why you guys gotta hassle him night and day. He ain't done nothing."

"We're here to take a quick look. If there are no violations of his parole, we'll leave you in peace," Jude said.

"You all should leave him in peace anyway. Don't you have any real criminals to go after?" Uncle Leonard spit.

"Is Kenny home now?"

"Nah. Left an hour or so ago."

"To go where?"

"The supermarket," Leonard sneered. "Check his parole officer's paperwork. He's cleared to grocery shop. Guy's not in prison anymore."

"We'll search the premises, then, and talk to him later."

Leonard glared. "You aren't going to search anything."

Jude grew a few inches taller. "Sir, I am not asking your permission. Please step aside. We'll make this as quick and painless as we can."

Leonard's gaze swept to the curb and found Beckett. It took him a moment, but then his eyes narrowed to furious slits. "Beckett Duke? That's the guy who should be in prison, right there. He killed my niece and he got off without paying his dues. Why don't you go drag him back to jail, where he belongs?"

Jude's tone was placating. "All we want to do is make sure Kenny doesn't have a weapon in the home. Then we'll head on over to the grocery store to find him. If he gets back here first, have him call me." Jude pulled a business card from his pocket. Leonard made no move to take it, so Jude wedged it behind the mailbox that was affixed to the wall of the trailer.

Leonard reached out and snatched up the card and then threw it on the ground. Both cops were on high alert as he began to rant again. Beckett's gaze drifted to a movement from the rear of the trailer. Someone was exiting through a window, someone long and lean, his blond hair grown out unevenly from a prison buzz cut. Kenny Sanderson.

Beckett's nerves kicked like a mule. "Stop, Kenny," he yelled.

Kenny dropped to the gravel below, knees bent and primed to run. A knife in a sheath was fastened to his belt. Beckett was already in motion, hollering to Jude and tearing after Kenny.

Kenny sprinted away from the trailer, toward the small fence that separated two yards. He leaped over it easily. Beckett pursued him, not nearly as deftly, but urgency fueled his big body up and over. Kenny raced through the yard, around a half-empty kids' wading pool, and ran full tilt through the open side gate. Beckett was closing the gap when Kenny jagged right. He flew between two trailers and out into the gravel parking area designated for visitors. Boots slipping on the rocky surface, Beckett did the same. Pushing hard, Beckett edged closer until his outstretched hand grazed the hood of Kenny's sweatshirt.

One more spurt of speed and he reached out again, snagging the cloth. Before he could reel Kenny to a stop, Beckett's foot dipped down into a hollow where the gravel had sunk into a crack in the parched ground. He went down and cartwheeled head over heels until he landed flat on his back, the breath forced out of him. Before he could clear the stars from his eyes, Kenny was on him, the knife pressed to his throat.

Kenny's pale eyes glittered, his breath hot in Beckett's face.

"Why, Beckett Duke, as I live and breathe. You decided to come to me so I could kill you easier? So thoughtful." Spittle formed on the edge of Kenny's lips.

"I came to watch you get taken back to prison," Beckett said between gasps.

"That's not gonna happen." He spoke through gritted teeth, the knife pressed into Beckett's throat. He felt a warm trickle of blood. "I'm the one who's laying down the law now and I've already told you how you're gonna pay for what you did to Pauline."

"I didn't kill your sister," Beckett grunted.

"Yes, you did." His mouth quivered. "Pauline didn't deserve what you did to her. She was a nurse. She took care of people, only one in my family who ever made something of herself. She tried so hard to straighten me out."

Beckett's body screamed at him to move, but he did not dare risk the knife digging any farther into his windpipe. "Pauline was dead when I found her."

"Shut your mouth. You don't even get to say her name. Only thing I can do for my sister now is make you pay."

"Leave my family alone."

Kenny's fingers pressed the knife harder. "I'm going to kill you, just like I promised." He leaned closer. His grin showed irregular front teeth. "But you're going to watch your wife die first." He laughed. "Hey, you know what? I heard someone in town blabbing away. So Mrs. Duke is expecting, huh?"

Beckett froze.

Kenny moved his face close to Beckett's until they were practically nose to nose. "My sister always wanted to have kids. *As soon as I have a baby, you can be Uncle Kenny*, she would tell me, but she never got the chance, and your wife isn't gonna get that chance either."

"Don't…" Beckett began, but Kenny cut him off.

"Congratulations, Daddy. Guess that's two people you'll be burying before you die."

Fury ignited Beckett's senses. He grabbed up a handful of gravel and flung it.

Kenny reared up. Beckett scrambled to his feet, but his balance was off and he staggered. He shook off the dizziness in time to see Kenny almost to the tree line, and three police cars approaching, lights and sirens clearing the way. Two officers peeled off, and Beckett knew they were heading for the opposite sides of the thicket where Kenny might be able to hitch a ride out of town. Jude stopped his vehicle and got out, talking urgently into his radio as he inspected Beckett.

Beckett stared at the woods, trying to rein in his surging emotions.

"You hurt?" Jude said.

"No."

Jude pulled a first-aid kit from his car and handed Beckett a gauze pad. "Blood usually indicates injury, but since you're standing and argumentative, I'll assume it's minor. I'm going to assist my officers."

Beckett swiped at his bloody neck. "He's got a knife, all right. I can confirm that."

Sliding behind the wheel, Jude said, "Good news is we can arrest him now, soon as we catch him, for a couple of violations now that he's attacked you."

"He reminded me of his promise to kill Laney before he finishes me off. He knows about the baby too."

Jude studied Beckett for a moment, his expression unreadable. "We'll get him." The radio crackled, indicating his partners had not yet located their quarry.

"So now you believe me that Kenny is a threat?" Beckett was three parts angry and one part relieved.

"Kenny's actions just bore out your story, so it's clear that he is hot on your trail. Chasing him didn't help your case, though. A lot of folks around here feel as though Kenny might be justified in his revenge on you."

Beckett felt the adrenaline that had swamped his body give way to a bone-deep weariness. "You too, Jude? You still think I killed his sister?"

"At first, I didn't have any doubts. We had evidence. Cousin or not, we had you for it. You admitted going to meet her. You had her sweater in your truck. Fibers from her clothes were under your fingernails."

"Like I said, I tried CPR." Beckett waited for the rest of whatever Jude had to say.

"Lately, though…" Jude shrugged. "I've been turning things over in my mind."

"And?"

"And I think it's possible you didn't mean to hurt her, something happened, things got out of control, might have been manslaughter, not murder."

Beckett could read the rest of Jude's thoughts. *Things got out of hand…like they did when you blinded Dan in the wrestling match.* The sense of defeat settled deeper into his soul. "Why would I do that, Jude? I hardly knew Pauline."

"You dated in high school your senior year. As I recall, she thought you were pretty hot stuff. She wanted to be your steady girlfriend, but you weren't interested in anything long-term. Had your sights on a sports scholarship. You brushed her off."

"That was a lifetime ago. I was arrogant, probably even an insensitive jerk about her feelings. I own all that, but that doesn't make me a killer."

Jude shrugged. "We had plenty of evidence to take you into custody."

"You never made a mistake before? Arrested someone who was innocent?"

Jude's badge shone in the sunlight, a blinding sheen. "No, Beckett. I haven't."

Whether it had been murder or involuntary manslaughter, his cousin still believed he'd killed Pauline, just like Kenny did. He would never change Jude's opinion. So be it. He wouldn't waste any more breath on it. There were more important issues at stake. "He's gonna hurt Laney. Aren't we on the same side here?"

"I'm on Laney's side."

"If you don't catch him quickly, he'll go after her."

Jude opened his door. "Wait here and I'll call someone to drive you to the clinic or your truck."

"I'll walk to my truck," Beckett said. "You've got a fugitive to catch." He didn't wait for Jude's answer. The cut on his throat stung, but that was the least of his concerns as he circled back around to his vehicle. Jude may have been confident that the police would capture Kenny, but Beckett did not share his rosy view. Kenny had a network of friends on both sides of the jail fence who would no doubt be happy to assist. He was so deep in his thoughts, he'd yanked open his driver's door before he noticed all four tires were flat, neatly slashed.

He scanned the street. Good old Uncle Leonard pulled back the shades of his house. He flashed Beckett a hateful grin and raked an index finger across his throat. No confusion about the meaning.

Beckett stared him down until Leonard

disappeared from the window. He kept his appearance calm as he took out his phone and called for a tow truck before he dialed Herm.

"Yello, Hotsprings Hotel," he said. "Help ya?"

"It's Beck. Is Laney okay?"

There was a brief pause and he heard the phone being handed off. "Yes, I am," she said. "Where are you?"

He tried to keep his relief silent. "I'm still in Beatty." He told her about the encounter with Uncle Leonard and Kenny's escape, leaving out the part about the knife at his throat. He heard her sharp intake of breath. "So stay in, okay?"

"I have to take the Timmons family and Rita into the park today at four. Levi's leading a trail ride and Willow's joining in at sundown on the nighttime photo tour if the sky is clear."

A long drive through one of the world's most desolate landscapes. Death Valley was a deadly place in the best of circumstances. "I'll take them."

"We'll talk about it later. I have to help serve breakfast." She paused. "Don't... I mean, you should be careful too, you know."

She still cared? He wished. "Right. I'll be back as soon as I get the tires replaced." He resisted the urge to order her to stay put again. Laney was not one to put up with badgering. *You said your piece.*

Still, the minutes passed in excruciating slowness until the tow driver arrived and hauled his truck to the local garage. The driver was new in town and wise enough not to inquire how Beckett had earned himself four slashed tires. He listened to his earbuds, ignoring Beckett in the passenger seat, which suited them both fine. Beckett had pulled on a windbreaker to hide the knife wound before the tow arrived, even though it was too hot for it.

At the garage, Beckett found fire captain Trent Clouder waiting by his staff vehicle for some paperwork. He was slender, belt buckled around a trim waist, hair neatly cut, boots polished to a sheen. Trent was probably close to sixty, but his commitment to working out and perhaps even tinting his hair made him appear younger. He'd been married and divorced twice.

The captain went slack jawed for a moment when he saw Beckett and then extended a hand. They shook.

"We miss you," Trent said. "You were the best volunteer this department's ever had."

They were the kindest words he'd heard in a long time. He sincerely hoped the captain wasn't just being patronizing. Trent had a golden tongue, as he'd heard Irene comment one time.

"I want to come back." Beckett hadn't meant to say it, but the longing to return to his duties, to regain the position that had provided him such satisfaction, overwhelmed his common sense. He'd dearly loved his days in the firehouse, tending to the machinery, cooking for the crew, riding on every imaginable type of call from car accidents to heat exhaustion.

Trent shifted, dark eyes wandering from

Beckett's face. "You know I'd like to do that," he said softly, "but it's a matter for the fire board. I'd put in a good word for you, of course."

And they would never approve his re-hire, not unless he was completely vindicated of the crime. Perhaps not even then. "I understand."

"You've been on my mind, actually. I was at the library last week doing a talk for the teen group and there was someone there asking Mrs. Shick about you."

Someone was asking the librarian about him? "Who?"

"Don't know her."

Her? "Can you tell me what she looked like?"

"Tall, dark hair pulled into a braid. Familiar description?"

He nodded. "Her name's Rita Brown. She's staying at the Hotsprings. What did Mrs. Shick tell her?"

Clouder laughed. "You know Mrs. Shick. She didn't get to be a captain in the army without having a spine made of steel. She told her she'd be delighted to help her find books, but for gossip she'd have to go elsewhere. The gal was nosy. Not nearly as warm and friendly as Pauline."

"I didn't know you and Pauline were close."

He lifted a shoulder. "Not really. I mean, I talked to her some, when she first came to town. She was in the coffee shop one time and I joined her. Just to be welcoming, you know."

Pauline was a striking woman. She'd been vivacious and popular in high school, active in dozens of clubs and an attendee at every dance. Some twenty-five years later when she'd checked in at the hotel, she'd been wary, reserved, a certain hesitation in her manner, but she was still a lovely woman and would have been noticed by a man like Trent.

"I figured I'd strike up a conversation with Rita at the library, but she brushed me off." He shrugged. "Not very friendly, like I said."

"Yeah."

Trent regarded him with a raised eyebrow. "So what's going on really? Why is this Rita in Furnace Falls, grilling people about you?"

"I would love to know," Beckett said. And he'd be sure to pass the info on to Jude.

Trent's radio squawked.

Beckett mouthed a "thank you" and went to pay for his new set of tires. He willed the minutes to pass quickly so he could get back to the hotel.

If Rita was a snake in their midst, he was going to be there to prevent her sinking her fangs into Laney.

SEVEN

Laney had polished the dining room tables after breakfast until they shone. The few guests still in attendance had already departed to take advantage of the relative cool. In the afternoon they would be returning to use the pool, nap or gather in the shade underneath the sprawling tree, recharging before their evening plans. Death Valley was a place where people structured their activity levels to match the most hospitable temperatures. There was really no other choice. She'd already added the important details to the chalkboard in the dining room: "sunup 6:19 a.m., sunset 7:14 p.m., high temperature 96. Stay hydrated!"

She'd first come to Las Vegas from Oregon when an acquaintance told her there were plenty of hotel jobs to be had. A flat-broke teenager, all alone, having recently lost her baby, she couldn't think of another plan. Climbing out of that bus, she'd thought the heat would cook her on the spot. She'd been trying hard not to cry when Aunt Kitty found her in the bus station.

"Where you headed to, hon?" she asked.

"Nowhere," she'd croaked. Aunt Kitty plopped down next to her, bought her a bottle of water and brought her home to Death Valley as if she were one of the brood, along with Jude and his absent sister, Sadie. It was Aunt Kitty who had found her work at the Hotsprings Hotel, the place where she'd met Beckett.

Determined not to fall into a nostalgic pit of despair, she finished wiping the table, which had housed the bacon, eggs and Herm's made-from-scratch blueberry muffins. Admiral happily snarfed up the crumbs that settled to the floor.

She headed to the oven to finish the oatmeal-raisin cookies that would go in the dinner pack for the evening tour. It was the first recipe Aunt Kitty had taught her, and one of the few that she could not possibly mess up. Herm sang from his repertoire of country songs while he delved into the commercial freezer to inventory the supplies. The kitchen was redolent with the smell of cinnamon. Her thoughts drifted to Beckett. Four tires would take a while to replace, so she was not surprised at his delay, but she found herself breathing easier when she heard his truck pull up.

He entered through the back kitchen door with all the delicacy of a tornado about to touch down. As he bent low to retrieve the napkins he'd knocked to the floor, she noted the tension in his tall frame. For some reason, he wouldn't look her directly in the eye.

He slouched against the kitchen counter, frowning.

"Sit down," she said. "You can sample

a cookie while you tell me all about what happened."

"I already…"

"I want to hear the whole story. You only gave me the highlights on the phone, I'm sure."

As he sat, she noticed the smear of blood on his throat. "Beckett," she cried, moving to him to peer closer.

"It's not bad."

She tipped his chin up. The strong curve of his jaw was so familiar and new at the same time. Clean-shaven, as he'd been every day since she'd known him, his skin was smooth under her touch. He was a paradox to her, meticulous about his grooming, couldn't stand his hair getting long enough to tickle his ears, yet completely oblivious about the hole in the knee of his jeans.

"Can I get a haircut appointment with my best gal?" he would call out, bursting through the back door of the hotel, heedless of the hour. She would laughingly shush him before she got out the electric shears and began her trimming. It was an effort, since he would try to steal kisses throughout the whole process.

Swallowing down the memories, she studied the wound. His face was so close, she could smell the clean scent of the locally made soap they supplied at the hotel. Her pulse ticked up. "The cut is long but not deep." She cupped his chin. "Tell me what happened right now or I'm calling Jude."

"Kenny went at me with a knife," Beckett said after a pause.

The breath crystallized in her lungs. For a moment, all she could do was stare into his brown irises, her own shock mirrored back at her. A knife, drawn across his throat. A fraction deeper and… Unfortunately, her eyes began to fill. Annoying hormones. She whirled away and retrieved the first-aid kit. With a shaking hand, she glided an alcohol-soaked cotton ball on the wound.

Beckett grimaced at the sting. "He

wasn't trying to kill me. If that was his goal, I'd be dead already."

"Why do I not find much comfort in that?" It occurred to her with a jolt that Beckett's death would mean her baby would be fatherless. But wasn't that what life would be like for the child anyway, after they divorced and Beckett made good on his promise to move away? Wasn't that what she wanted? She stood frozen, clutching the cotton.

He reached up and circled her wrist. "Kenny's got something else in mind." He paused. "He wants to hurt you because he knows that would be the worst thing that could ever happen to me."

She stilled. This time, she could not hide her tears. No words were necessary; she was sure he could read her thoughts like he'd been able to do most of the time they'd known each other. *No one could hurt me worse than you did.*

She allowed his hands to circle her waist, spanning the growing life inside her. For a moment, she could almost pretend he was still the loving man who had committed before God to stay by her side.

For better or for worse… The muscles worked in his throat, pain etched in the lines around his mouth. Pain? He had no idea how much pain he had unleashed in her heart. All this protectiveness now was too late. The throb of tenderness turned bitter.

He'd quit on their marriage, quit on her. She stepped back, freeing herself from his grasp.

She blinked furiously, snatched up another cotton ball and finished disinfecting the wound in silence, applying antibiotic ointment as a final step. "That should heal up okay now. You won't even have a scar."

"Thank you." He sat back in the chair. "There's something else. I found out Rita has been asking in town about me."

Laney jerked. "Our guest Rita? Why would she do that?"

"I don't know, but I am going to find out. She's not what she seems to be. I don't want you around her."

Laney bit back her irritation but some leaked into her words anyway. "That's all well and good for you to make pronouncements like that, but there are commitments that need keeping, tours that were paid for. Like I told you, I have to take her and the Timmons family into the park in a couple of hours. This is supposed to be our busy season. We aren't in a position to issue refunds or withstand the angry reviews they will post on Yelp if we cancel on them."

"I'll drive them."

"Which will leave me here alone, since Levi is leading the horse tour."

"Herm...?"

"Is on his way to get lumber to fix the chicken coop. He's already cooked the roast for the couple of families who we are blessed enough to have staying here still. It's in the warming oven for me to put out."

Beckett considered, standing and staring through the cheerful checked curtains.

"All right," he said finally. "We'll go together, then."

Together. That was occurring entirely too much in the last few days. With her emotions zinging around the place like dust in a whirlwind, it did not seem to her a very wise idea to spend hours in close contact with Beckett. But there was no help for it. She bent to toss the cotton in the wastebasket, staggering a little when she straightened until he bolted over and pulled her close.

"What is it? Are you all right? Sit down. I'll get water. Should I call the doctor?" The stream of panicked questions continued until she pressed a finger to his lips.

"Shush. It's okay. I just get dizzy sometimes if I stand too quickly. Irene says it's perfectly normal. Everything is fine. I just haven't had enough water lately probably…"

In a flash, he was pressing her into the chair he'd vacated and striding to the sink. In ten seconds she had a large glass of water in her hand. "Drink."

She sipped, figuring compliance was the best way to get him to leave.

"Drink more."

She complied with an eye roll.

"I think you should finish the whole thing."

"My bladder isn't that big and I've got a baby taking up real estate in there too, so ease up, would you?"

To her surprise, he laughed. The sound was rich and sonorous, and it momentarily took her breath away. There had been so much laughter in this very kitchen... The time he'd baked her a birthday cake and dropped it, the day they'd rescued a squirrel that had been hit by a car and promptly revived in time to lead them on a merry chase. There had been a bounty of blessings that she'd thought would be hers forever...until the moment Pauline's body was found. Again she felt the tears threaten, and she forced them back.

Beckett's laughter died away, but his smile was still in full force. "How about just a few small sips, until little Muffin simmers down?"

She arched a brow. "Muffin? Does that work for both genders?"

He gulped. "It just, you know, popped into my mind. Do you...? I mean, do you have a guess about the gender?"

Why did the question stab right to her heart? "If the Lord gives me a healthy baby, it doesn't matter to me."

He looked pained. "Me too. I..." He trailed off.

"What?"

He looked down, and she was startled to catch the glimmer of moisture in his eyes. "Nothing."

Something inside made her whisper. "Tell me."

"I know the baby will have the best mother in the world..." he choked out. "But why me for a father?"

The moment stretched taut as a wire between them. She'd spent four months wondering what God was up to, granting her heart's desire at the moment her life cracked into millions of jagged pieces.

"I don't know why, Beckett, why now, why us, but I can tell you there is no part of this baby that isn't God breathed and God blessed. If I can just..." Her voice caught, and she clamped her lips shut. What had happened to her ability to control her tongue?

He was quiet for several seconds. "If you can carry the baby to term?" he finished for her.

How could he still read her so easily? It was not fair.

She squeezed her hands together. "I made bad choices in the past, but I know God has forgiven me. He's blessed me beyond measure with this pregnancy and I trust Him. It's just that sometimes when I consider all that's happened, with us, and Pauline, it reminds me how easily blessings can be stripped away."

He nodded. "It must have been a shock to find out that you were pregnant."

"It was the second-best day of my life," she said.

And the first? He didn't ask because he already knew. As a matter of fact, it was engraved inside the wedding ring she no longer wore. *Our wedding day, our future.* It was written in his too, and she noticed he still wore his. She was unsure how she should feel about that.

He cleared his throat and walked to the door. "I, uh… I'm going to go check on some things."

She nodded, relieved that he would leave her in peace to deal with a stomach suddenly gone unsettled.

"What room is Rita's?" he asked.

"It's…" Shock slammed into her.

"What's wrong?"

She felt cold all over. "Something just occurred to me."

He waited.

"Rita Brown."

"What about her?"

"She's staying in Room 205," she said, around a lump in her throat.

He stared. "She's in the room Pauline stayed in?"

Laney nodded.

"Did that happen randomly?"

Slowly, she shook her head. "No. I remembered just now. When she made the reservation, she asked specifically for that room. She said a friend of her family had stayed there before and she knew it was a good room." Why hadn't she noticed that odd fact before? Rita had asked specifically to stay in the same room as the murdered Pauline Sanderson.

A chill wave passed through her body, rippling her skin. She looked to Beckett, hoping there would be something in his glance that would reassure her that it was strange coincidence.

But Beckett's demeanor told her nothing of the kind. He knew, and she knew, that something was wrong about Rita— very wrong.

Beckett clicked off the phone again. He'd left two messages for Jude, neither

of them returned. In retrospect, he probably shouldn't have made them sound quite
so much like demands. *What is the status
with Kenny? You need to investigate Rita
Brown.* He wished he could erase the messages and try again. That was the problem,
Beckett thought. When would he learn
that asking and telling were two different things? Reflexively, he bent his head
to pray and then stopped himself. What
was the point of that? Laney often would
ask him to pray with her, and he'd always
declined. Something about the vulnerability of it made him squirm. God didn't
want to hear his woes and it was embar-
rassing to give them an audible voice. In
jail he'd given it up altogether. If God was
listening, Beckett wouldn't have been imprisoned in the first place.

He shoved his phone into his pocket and
spent time pulling up a warped floorboard
in one of the unoccupied tent units. Practically all of them were unoccupied. Maybe
when he'd left Furnace Falls, potential vis-

itors would forget there had been a murder on the premises.

How much time would that take?

After he plucked a sliver out of his thumb and returned the hammer to the toolbox, he lent a hand packing the van and stationing himself there to prevent anyone from adding or subtracting any items. There was no way there would be any intruders this time, reptilian or otherwise.

He sat on the bumper waiting for his opportunity. Rita's door opened. She shouldered a backpack, a camera in her other hand. The Timmons family was still gathered on the porch, doling out water bottles and snacks for each person. They were appropriately dressed, he was happy to note, with full sun protection and windbreakers in case of a rain shower. Sturdy shoes, faces shiny with sunscreen.

Rita too was clad for the adventure, in jeans and a T-shirt, with a canary yellow slicker tied around her waist. So as not to spook her, he waited until she approached.

"Oh, hi," she said. "Are you our driver now too?"

"Yes." He paused for a beat. "I figure you'll have plenty of time to ask me questions directly, instead of interviewing people in town."

She shrugged. "Small-town scandal is interesting, and I'm a curious person."

"Me too. I'm curious about why you requested Room 205."

She went still. "A family friend..."

He held up a palm. "Spare me. How about the real reason?"

Laney walked toward him, her wary glance darting between the two of them. The breeze blew her oversize shirt taut over her stomach, outlining the slight swell of her abdomen. A baby, their baby. He had to force himself to concentrate.

Rita unwrapped a stick of gum and put it in her mouth. She nodded to Laney. "I'll be ready to go as soon as I finish enduring this interrogation."

"I'm sorry. We don't mean to offend." She tugged the shirt straight.

"I was politely asking why she wanted to stay in Room 205," Beckett said.

"The truth is exactly what I said, about my family friend who stayed in the unit," Rita said.

Laney stepped in before Beckett could answer. "Please, Rita," she said quietly. "We've been through a nightmare and all we want is to get on with our lives. The truth...that's all we want to know."

Rita's mouth pursed for a long moment and something seemed to give inside her. "All right." She tipped her chin up. "I'm a reporter. I'm writing a story about what happened to Pauline."

A reporter...all they needed. He resisted the urge to groan aloud. "For what paper?"

"An online publication."

"Which one?"

She was about to answer when Mrs. Timmons rallied her family to start walking to the van. The teens were in the middle of a noisy squabble.

Another interruption, a further delay in getting the real story. Or had he gotten it already? Was she really a journalist reviving a story? She'd rake him through the mud again, but that was preferable to thinking she was in league with Kenny.

Truth or lies?

Was Rita a nosy nuisance? There was way too much at stake.

Keep your guard up, Beckett.

EIGHT

Laney sat in the passenger spot, Beckett behind the wheel. Rita had been only too happy to climb into the middle row seat with Mrs. Timmons. Mr. Timmons sat strategically in the rear between his sons, who both stared stonily at their cell phones. She watched the scenery pass by without feeling the usual rush of pleasure as they crested the Funeral Mountains and dropped down into the area where they would meet Levi at the Keane Wonder Mine. Though Mr. and Mrs. Timmons kept up a sporadic conversation, remarking on the variety of colors the waning sun teased from the rocks, the van was mostly quiet.

"Your visit is well-timed," Laney said,

putting on her tour-guide hat. "The mine was closed by the National Park Service for several years to make it safer."

"How?" said Mrs. Timmons.

"They covered over some exposed mine entrances and shored up the old structures." She did not add that mines seemed to be magnets for exploration and more than one thrill seeker had lost their lives.

They rumbled into the parking area, and the guests were freed from the vehicle. Rita and Mr. and Mrs. Timmons gazed up at the lower tramway, the rickety wooden artifact protruding from the golden rock like some sort of giant metal insect. The mine had produced a staggering amount of gold in its time. There were plenty of weathered relics dotting the scarred rock, but most visitors wanted to see the impressive aerial tramway towers and terminals, which required a steep mile-long hike.

Levi was already there. He met them with a quiet "hello." The horses were saddled, tails swishing. The trailer would have already been dropped at their end point by a stable hand. The teen boys perked up from their sullen contemplation at the sight of the horses. Laney hid her smile at the joy that lit their faces. She wanted to shake them and say, "You have two parents who love you. Don't you know how precious that is? Put down your phones and revel in it."

Laney had been taken from her drug-addicted mother as a toddler and had landed in the foster care system. The family who she'd finally settled with at age eight was supportive, but not particularly warm. She'd mistaken that support for love. After their biological daughter went off to college, they'd summarily asked Laney to leave when she turned eighteen. It had started a tailspin that had taken years, and the timely rescue from Aunt Kitty, to save her from.

"Awesome," one of the teens said, pulling her from her reverie.

After Levi delivered a quick safety-and animal-behavior lesson, Rita and the family mounted their horses. Levi waved at Beckett and Laney. "Meet you later." He guided the eager visitors along a narrow trail.

She sighed. Now she would be left alone with Beckett to make their way to the Harmony Borax Works and wait until the guests arrived for dinner. Though she was glad not to be in the saddle in the hot remnants of the day, it was still going to be a long couple of hours. What in the world were they supposed to talk about?

Beckett was silent the first few miles and she kept her gaze fixed solidly out the side window.

"Do you believe her?" he said abruptly.

"Rita?" Laney mulled it over. "I'm not sure. Do you?"

"No, but I don't believe much of anyone. In jail, the only way to stay alive was to distrust everyone."

"I think that started before jail." She regretted her words immediately.

He shot her a look. "How do you mean?"

Why not tell him? He would be stepping

out of her life anyway. "High school, what happened in the wrestling match… I think that might have been when you changed."

He shifted. "The world changed. It was like everyone suddenly saw me differently after what happened with Dan, like I was a bad person."

"And you started seeing yourself that way."

He shrugged.

"Aunt Kitty told me one time it was like you began to believe what your naysayers said. Their labels became your identity."

"I… I ruined Dan's life. Hard to forget that."

"Dan Wheatly is a successful man, a practicing attorney." Who had, in fact, reached out to contact Beckett a few times, but Beckett had left the phone calls unanswered.

He shook his head. "Let's not go into that."

Laney sighed. Some things had not changed, no matter how many times she'd prayed about them.

Beckett went on. "I'd feel better if Jude could confirm some facts for us. He'll call when he can."

"Do you think they've caught Kenny?"

He didn't reply, which was answer enough. Kenny was still out there somewhere, planning his next move. They arrived at the Harmony Borax Works.

Beckett unfurled the pop-up canopy and set up a folding table underneath. Laney spread it with a gingham tablecloth and set out plates, cups, insulated pitchers of ice water and lemonade. She checked on the tamale casserole, still warm in the baking dish, and the side salads, chilling in their second cooler. They used to provide a cut of beef, cooked on a portable grill right on the spot. After Beckett went to jail, Laney had incinerated several rib-eye steaks before she hung up her tongs and switched to casseroles.

It was nearing seven now, and the sun sank into a bronze puddle behind the crumbling brick building. William Coleman, who'd built the facility in the 1800s, had found the Death Valley temperatures to be a struggle too. When the processing water was too hot to allow the borax to crystallize, he moved operations. The only animals strong enough to haul the borax to the new site were mules, and the legendary 20 Mule Team Borax was born.

Laney had always loved the story, romanticizing the crumbling brick structures, imagining she could hear the long-ago braying of the rugged animals. At the moment, the quiet struck her as sinister. Shadows gobbled up the landscape. But the old borax works were the perfect place for stargazing and a starting spot for the night photo activity Willow would conduct. Though the temperatures had only just begun to dip back down into the high seventies, she put on her sweater anyway. Pulling the lighter from her pocket, she lit the small oil lantern. No one used oil lanterns anymore, but she loved the old thing she'd found in the basement and it set just the right tone in this aged place.

When Beckett's phone vibrated, the

quiet noise made her jump. He put it on Speaker. "Laney and I are here, Jude. Go ahead."

"Here where?"

"In the park, borax works, waiting for the hotel guests."

Jude paused. "Kenny got past us."

Beckett's knuckles whitened on the phone. "How?"

Jude's tone was defensive. "Any number of ways, but we don't think he's left the area. I had roadblocks in place immediately, so he's found someplace to hole up. Maybe doubled back to town and called on a friend. We're canvassing. We'll find him."

"He'll call his uncle for money, supplies," Beckett snapped.

"Got that angle covered already, Beckett. They taught us that in cop school. We have an officer watching the trailer."

Laney jumped in quickly. "Jude, Beckett said he told you that Rita has been asking about him."

His voice gentled. "Yes. I've been looking into her, after Beckett called me. Sorry it's taken me a while. She doesn't have a record. She writes for an online newspaper."

Laney caught Beckett's eye. So she'd been telling the truth. The tension in her stomach let go a notch. "She said she was doing an article on Pauline's murder."

"That's outside her wheelhouse," Jude said. "She does the fluff stuff—community events, gardening tips and the like. Not investigative pieces."

"Maybe she's looking to switch gears?" Laney suggested. "Make a name for herself?"

"Possible. I'll continue to dig and see what I can unearth."

Beckett pulled in a breath. "I...uh... Thank you. For checking her out. I really appreciate it."

Laney was surprised by Beckett's humility. She added her own thanks. At least they could take Rita off the suspect list. She might be hankering to write an exposé to lift herself up the ladder, but that wasn't a crime. "Thanks for calling, Jude."

But he wasn't finished. "But there's one more thing you should know. Rita's hometown… It's Baileyville, Oregon."

The headline flashed into Laney's brain. Nurse from Small Oregon Town Slain in Death Valley. Though she'd tried hard not to read the avalanche of articles, she'd not been able to avoid them all. She remembered a few of the details. Pauline Sanderson, age forty-two, was a sports enthusiast who played on the Baileyville Broncos soccer team.

She sank down on a folding chair. "You mean Rita is from the same town as Pauline?"

"Yes."

She could see the shock on Beckett's features. "Did they know each other?"

"I haven't found any connection so far other than the hometown as of yet."

Beckett thanked him and hung up.

They sat in silence for a while, watching the flickering lantern flame. Beckett cracked his knuckles, a habit that used to drive her to distraction.

"There is something going on here that we haven't figured out yet," he said.

"It could be there's nothing sinister in it. Rita knew about Pauline's murder because she worked for a paper in the same hometown. That's what sparked her interest in the first place."

"She didn't mention it. My gut tells me there's more to her story."

"I agree." She shoved her hands in her pockets. "What do you think we should do?"

"Let Jude continue his investigation, and work on one of our own." He looked hastily at her. "Me, I mean. Not you. You should…"

She sighed. "I know. Stay in my room with Admiral and eat bonbons."

He laughed and pointed to her belly. "Does Muffin like bonbons?"

She gave him an arch look. "I am dead certain that Muffin will have the good sense to appreciate fine chocolate."

The corner of his mouth lifted. "I'll have to ask at the chocolate shop for some, those lemon-cream-filled ones you like."

She felt her cheeks heat. "I didn't think you'd remember that."

"Honey, after you ate the first one, you looked like you'd been given all the secrets of the universe."

Honey... She allowed a smile. "Only the important ones."

He looked away suddenly as if it pained him too much. "Yeah," he said so softly she almost didn't hear, "I will never forget the bliss on your face right then."

Her cheeks went hot, and she was grateful that the growing darkness hid her from his sight. A snap sounded somewhere behind them, and they both tensed.

A jackrabbit darted across the landscape, enormous ears primed for danger. She exhaled. Eyes wide and leaping at every shadow, she reckoned she was beginning to understand how the poor things must feel.

"I'll be right back." Beckett slunk into

the darkness, walking to a high point so he could view the road in the distance.

But surely Kenny could not have found them. How would he know where they were? Nowhere on their website did they provide a schedule of their evening tours. Beckett had even made her take down the photo gallery of their previous tours, in case Kenny or anyone else was trying to reconstruct their regular excursions. The breeze borne across the dry ground should have been refreshing, but it felt too chill and she clamped her arms around her body.

Several long minutes passed until Beckett returned and sat in a chair. "No sign of anyone." He patted her hand.

Without realizing it, she had eased her folding chair closer to his. Determinedly, she edged it away. She would not give him any false signals.

When the silence between them became too awkward, she checked on the food again. The soft pool of golden light from the lantern cheered her.

Levi arrived, leading the small party of riders behind him. The guests appeared to be pleased with the first part of their adventure, chattering and pointing. They dismounted and cleaned their hands with the wet towels she provided, exclaiming over the drama of the abandoned borax mine on the horizon. Rita did not join in the conversation, instead checking her cell phone.

"No service out here," Beckett told her. "Gotta have a satellite phone. Mountain walls are too high."

"No problem," she said. She took a seat and unfurled the napkin in her lap, draining half her glass of ice water.

Laney was happy to be busy serving up the meal, which was devoured in no time. Levi, as usual, picked at his food and passed up the dessert entirely. Everyone else ate hearty portions of the casserole and several of the oatmeal-raisin cookies she'd toted along. Willow arrived, her strawberry hair refusing to stay contained in her hair band. She drove a Jeep with the back end loaded with several tripods and extra cameras.

She swept a hand up at the sheen of stars beginning to reveal themselves in the sky. "No moon and clear skies. The perfect night for starwatching," she said grandly. Willow's effervescent personality could not be further removed from her nearly silent brother. "Who's ready to take some one-of-a-kind photos? We'll just drive right over that ridge and you will see stars you can't believe are real."

She wasn't exaggerating. With no light pollution, the pitch-black canvas would come alive with a breathtaking show of constellations. Beckett had taken her to see them when they'd first started dating. She'd been rendered speechless by the magnificence. They'd shared their first kiss under the stars.

Now wasn't the time to wallow in memories. She packaged the leftover food and blew out the lantern.

The teens grabbed extra cookies from the plate and headed to the Jeep. She was glad to see that they seemed to have come out of their surly teenage shells. They were just as eager as their parents to dive into the next phase. Death Valley had a way of inspiring awe in any age group.

Levi loaded up the horse trailer. Beckett helped until all six horses were securely aboard. Levi bade the guests good-night as they piled into the Jeep. With Beckett out of earshot, Levi spoke softly to her.

"You gonna be okay here?" The unspoken part of his question was "...*with Beckett*?"

What could possibly be awkward about being in such a romantic location, awash in painful memories, with the man who no longer wanted to be married to her? Part of her wished she could ride with Levi back to the hot springs. Instead she nodded. "Yes, thanks, Levi. We'll clean up and head straight back home."

He saluted her with a finger to his cap and drove the trailer away, loosing a cloud of dust that mingled with the night air. Beckett was already packing the dirty dishes in a tub they reserved for the job. While she gathered up the linens, he stowed the table in the van, and shut the rear doors as his phone rang again.

He answered, his eyes rounding. "Herm? Calm down. Tell me again."

Laney waited, heart thumping. Whatever it was, it wasn't good.

Beckett was still listening while he spoke to her. "Laney, get in the van, okay? We have to go now."

She turned to get in. "Why? What's wrong?"

He disconnected and shoved the phone into his pocket.

A glare of headlights blinded her. She threw up a hand to shield her eyes. A vehicle hurtled toward them at breakneck speed, tires crunching over the sandy ground.

There was no more time to ask questions. He pushed her toward the safety of their van.

"Run, Laney!"

She tripped and went down on one knee.

Grabbing her hand, he urged her up. She got her feet under her and began to sprint. He pounded along right next to her.

The car accelerated as it bore down on them.

NINE

Laney ran in a blind panic toward the van. Her shoes skidded and slipped on the grit. The vehicle behind jolted across the ground, eating up the distance between them. It was coming so fast. Headlights scoured the night and the wheels sent vibrations into the ground that invaded her body. The revving engine sounded like the growl of a metal predator. Pain hitched her side, but she kept on running. If they could get to the van, crank the key she'd left in the ignition... They needed a minute, nothing more.

Feet flying, she ran faster until her breath was coming in shallow gasps and her pulse pounded. She risked another quick look over her shoulder. The four-door car was so close now she could make out the driver behind the wheel, a baseball cap pulled down low. Kenny? A scream bubbled up in her throat as she saw the front bumper pull closer. With a cry of despair she tried to speed up, but her body simply would not cooperate. The slight dips and swells in the dry earth threatened to trip her.

Cold sweat bathed her neck. Even through her panicked haze some part of her brain processed the truth: they would not make it to the van in time.

They were going to be run down; there was no escape. As if living a nightmare, she imagined the machine plowing into her, snapping her bones as if they were made of dry twigs. The impact would shatter her body, but what about the tiny life nestled deep down inside her? Buffered by only a fragile nest of flesh, would he or she survive? *You're not going to kill my baby.* The thought fueled her aching limbs and spurred her to take more gulps into her burning lungs. Leaning forward, she forced herself to her absolute limit, praying she would not step into a hole that would send her tumbling under the on-coming wheels. They would make it— they had to.

The engine snarled, moving ever closer, mocking her efforts. Pain flared in her side, a spark that fledged into fiery agony. She began to slow. *No, please...* she thought, willing herself to keep going in spite of her body's protests. The Hotsprings van was so close now she could see the dust collected on the windows. Three more yards, two. If they could only reach it.

But she could push herself no faster, and their pursuer was gaining speed. It was futile. The car was nearly upon them. Any moment she would feel the impact of the metal, cutting into her, into them, even while their eyes were fixed on the means of their escape. Still, she kept running, too scared to stop, too winded to scream. The car was so close she could feel the heat from the engine on her back.

Abruptly, Beckett grabbed her arm and

pulled her to the side. They tumbled together in a tangle of limbs until they came to a stop. Head still spinning, she watched as the car continued straight ahead and smashed front first into the rear of their van. Glass spewed in all directions. Metal crumpled with a squeal that drowned out her own scream. She got to her knees, gasping for breath. They were alive. She hugged herself in disbelief, but Beckett was urging her up.

"Keep going. Don't stop."

"I can't..." she panted.

"We have to run to the ruins," he commanded. "Come on. I'll help you."

The ruins? She thought she'd heard him wrong. Why would they do such a foolish thing? The old borax works were unstable, treacherous piles of loose brick concealed by the pitch dark. No lights, not even security lights, were permitted in the area to prevent light pollution. It would be a broken leg waiting to happen, or worse. She tried to stop and question him, but he was still gripping her hand.

The sound of shifting gears caught her attention. She managed to turn her head, and over his shoulder, she saw the car reversing, pulling free from the wrecked van with the sound of shearing metal that set her teeth on edge.

Horror nearly overwhelmed her. The nightmare was not over. He was still coming for them. She saw through dazed eyes that the car was turning now, correcting course, locking on their location.

She had no more breath left to scream as they ran for the ruined buildings perched at the top of a shallow slope. Despair roiled through her along with the fatigue. She didn't see what difference it would make. How long could they hide in a place that was no more than a series of exposed, disconnected segments of wall, without even a roof? Their pursuer would not give up, she was sure now, but her body craved shelter, anything that would protect them from being crushed under the wheels of the oncoming car. Helpful or not, the crumbling walls offered the faintest hope and she would grab at it.

Exhaustion began to strip away her speed. All her power of concentration was not enough to override her physical limitations. Her legs trembled. "Beckett," she tried to call out, but she could not make a sound.

He seemed to sense her struggle anyway. In one quick movement, he swept her up and kept going.

She wanted to protest, but it was as if her muscles had diverted all their power into keeping her heart pumping and her lungs working. Onward they hurried, Beckett's boots digging into the flaked rock. She closed her eyes to keep from being overwhelmed by dizziness.

She felt him setting her on her feet at the base of the plateau where the borax plant stood in all its decaying glory. The walkway up to the top was buttressed on either side by worn stone walls. They raced through the low split-rail fence and up the walkway. From the parking area below, brakes squealed and the car skidded to a halt, spitting a shower of gravel into the air; the stones prickled the back of her neck.

Beckett hustled her forward behind the nearest wall and then deeper into the shadowed interior. Inside there was a smell of desiccated earth. Dust swirled under their feet. With only a sliver of moon, the stones reflected the weak starlight. How many times had she brought guests to these ruins, thrilled to share with them the fascinating facts about the early mining history of Death Valley? Now the derelict structure was their one slim hope of survival.

Beckett stumbled over a jagged row of broken bricks, caught himself and plunged them deeper into the pitch dark. He muffled a cry when his shoulder impacted a protruding shard of brick. They had to move slower now to avoid breaking their ankles, ducking under pale archways to prevent cracking their skulls. She had never been able to adjust well to night vision, for all the evening hikes she and Beckett had taken in their happier days.

You gotta allow your eyes to get used to the dark, he'd say, and inevitably she'd answer with, *This is as good as they get.* He would laugh, tuck her arm under his and lead her back to the comfort of their little cabin.

Now she clung to his hand, stumbling after him like a blindfolded person navigating an obstacle course. She could hear nothing but her own harsh panting, the hammering of the blood through her veins. Her mouth had gone sand dry.

He kept pulling her along through passages she could barely see, over obstacles that tripped her up. Something scuttled under her feet. A tarantula? A rat?

They hurried to the far edge of the ruins where an old iron stove stood sentinel, its long, slender gooseneck chimney thrusting into the starlit sky. He stopped and they squatted there, the cold metal pressed against her lower back, momentarily screened from their pursuer. She tried hard to get her breathing under control so the dizziness would subside.

He bent close to her ear. "Do you have your phone?" he whispered.

"Yes." She could only make out the barest gleam of his face, the feel of his mouth near her temple.

"Take this." From his back pocket he pulled a water bottle he'd stuck there after dinner. He unscrewed the cap and offered it, but her hands shook too much, so he held it to her lips until she sipped. The water was warm, but it revived her. She waved him away, determined to grasp what he was saying. He capped the bottle and shoved it in her sweater pocket.

"You need to get out of here. Duck under the fence and run toward the road. Call Jude as soon as you think it's safe enough."

She thought she'd misheard him. The temperature seemed to plummet ten degrees as a chill enveloped her. Run away and leave him there? "What are you going to do?"

"Draw his attention and buy you time."

She shook her head. "No, Beckett."

He was peering around the edge of the stove. Below they heard a door slam. Kenny was coming for them. Time was running out. Beckett stared into the darkness, probably trying to gauge next steps.

"Beckett." She tugged on his sleeve until he turned to face her again. "I'll call for help right now."

"He'll hear you."

"We can split up, maybe knock him out or something, or try to get back to the van."

He didn't answer, merely shook his head and pointed her toward the fence that outlined the self-guided walk around the mine. "Go as fast as you can. If you can't flag down a car along the road, start walking. Get away, far away. Call Willow to come and get you."

The trembling in her limbs started up again. "Kenny's probably armed. He'll kill you."

"If he manages, it's going to be the hardest thing he ever does in his entire miserable life."

His tone was flat and hard as granite, and it scared her more than his words. "No," she said, using her "put-my-foot-down voice," trying to grab for his hand. Her stern tone was offset by an ill-timed wash of tears. Why now? Beckett wasn't her soul mate anymore, but she could not stand to think of harm coming to him.

His smile was almost undetectable in the darkness. He touched two fingers lightly to her belly for the briefest of moments. "Muffin's been through enough tonight."

Baby or no baby, he was not going to distract her with sweet talk. "Listen to me. Please. This isn't smart."

His chuckle was soft, almost inaudible. "Nobody ever accused me of being smart." He kissed her on the forehead.

"Beckett," she said, trying to hold on to his shirt to keep him from going.

He pressed another kiss to her hand. Without thinking, she turned so that her fingers were cupping his cheek. She felt rather than heard his sigh, the soft of his lips nuzzling her palm. For a moment, perhaps it was a trick of the starlight, she thought he looked younger, as he might have been before that tragic high school wrestling match.

"Go," he said, one more time before he vanished into the shadows.

Beckett crept back toward the center of the ruins, filling his palm with stones as he went. Sheltering behind a rusted ore cart, he listened. At first there was nothing except the sound of the wind riffling the bits of detritus along the base of the old structure. Then he caught sound of a cautious footfall. The noise ceased abruptly. Kenny was tracking him too.

Palming a couple of stones, he waited two counts. He hurled them in the direction of the old twenty-mule-team wagon perched to the side of the ruins, a source of fascination for scores of travelers every season. The rocks landed in a quiet patter, but it was enough. The footsteps stopped.

Beckett counted silently to five and then launched a second stone, which pinged off the rear wagon wheel.

A tiny light flicked to life, enough that Beckett caught a second of Kenny's profile before he smothered his phone against his chest. *Found you.* Wary as a cat on the hunt, Kenny moved several feet away from Beckett, skirting the ruined wall, still unaware of Beckett's position. The sight of Kenny standing there after he'd nearly killed them sent a hot streak of anger ripping through him.

Because of Kenny, his pregnant wife was running through the desert, where a host of additional threats might harm her. The land surrounding the borax works was riddled with potential hazards: snakes, heat… She could fall, become dehydrated, lost… The list ballooned in his mind along with the ire. Jaw tight, he kept his thoughts from those scenarios and forced himself to breathe slowly through his nose. He had to keep it together and deal with Kenny.

Kenny moved a step forward, close enough that Beckett caught the smell of cigarettes.

Everything in him wanted to hurtle out of his hiding place and crush Kenny into the sandy ground. Instead he bent and picked up another rock. All he had to do was play the diversion game long enough for Laney to get away. Just like firefighting... Move the victim to safety and then deal with everything else.

Give her another few minutes. When Kenny took a step to his right, Beckett readied his rock. He intended to land the rock on the other side of the wagon to mimic movement, but as soon as the pebble left his fingertips, Kenny jerked the light in Beckett's direction.

Before Beckett could work out what to do next, Kenny lunged, the knife flashing in his hand. There was nowhere to hide.

Beckett had one second to grab at Kenny's outthrust wrist to keep the blade from ripping into his abdomen. They went over backward, banging into the half-buried rocks, rolling over and over. Dust filled Beckett's mouth and stung his eyes as they struggled.

Kenny dug his elbow into Beckett's chest. Beckett's muscles locked tight as he held fast to Kenny's wrist, but he knew he could not sustain the effort indefinitely. Kenny was younger and stronger, and he had not just run at breakneck speed to escape a car bearing down on him. Painstakingly, he freed his leg just enough. With a sudden motion, he rammed his knee into Kenny's stomach. The breath whooshed out, followed by a grunt, and the knife spiraled away into the darkness. Both men scrambled up.

Kenny panted, bent at the waist, head angled to keep Beckett in sight.

Beckett's breath was ragged too as he squared off. "No knife now, Kenny. Got any guts without it?"

Kenny swiped at a dribble of blood on his chin. "Just as much as you had when you killed my sister with your bare hands.

Did it make you feel like a man to kill her, tough guy?"

"I didn't..." Beckett broke off. It was a waste of effort trying to explain the truth again. Eyes on his opponent, he circled around until he could flick a glance toward the wide flat of desert beyond. Had Laney gotten away? He saw no sign of headlights on the road, but maybe she must have been able to place a call to Jude with his satellite phone, and maybe one to his cousin. Willow would only be twenty minutes away with the tour group by now. Maybe she had already started back.

Kenny eased off a few steps. Retreating? Beckett didn't think so. Kenny flicked a glance at his phone, reading the screen before his gaze locked on Beckett.

What was going on? He remembered Rita's attention to her cell phone after she'd returned from the horseback ride. "Getting a text from your pal Rita?"

Kenny's chin went up. "Who?" Too late.

"You know her, don't you?" He was deciding on his next question when Kenny put his head down and barreled toward him like a freight train. He wheeled back, sliding on the uneven surface, and went down on one knee. It was the opening Kenny needed to slam him backward. Beckett's shoulders hit the rail fence. Wood fractured under his weight, and he tumbled through, cartwheeling down the slope until he landed at the bottom on hard-packed ground.

He was up again in a moment, hands fisted, ready for Kenny's next assault. Pain throbbed in his ribs, and he felt dizzy, but he shook the feelings off. "Come on down here, Kenny," he shouted. "We can go another round. As many as you want."

But Kenny didn't follow, staring down at Beckett. Was he pulling a gun? There was no place for Beckett to go. A gun would mean game over for him…but not for Laney. He tensed as Kenny cocked his head as if he was waiting.

Something was wrong. There was a detail he'd overlooked. What was it? What message had Kenny gotten on his phone?

"What are you waiting for?" he hollered. "Don't want to get your clothes dirty?"

A scream cut the darkness. Beckett's soul split in two as he realized it was Laney.

Kenny laughed, tipped his face up to the sky and chortled.

Beckett finally understood his own stupidity.

While he had been trying to buy time, so had his opponent.

Kenny had not come alone.

TEN

Laney's scream echoed across the flat ground, shrill and sharp. The hulking shadow some fifty yards behind her seemed to have appeared out of nowhere, materialized from the sand itself.

It was not Beckett; the silhouette was too short, too wide. She did not think it was Kenny either, from how Beckett had described him. There was no shouted offer of help, no attempt at introductions from the stranger, just the relentless, steady progress of the heavy booted feet. No engine noise indicated he'd emerged from a car, and the long, lonely road wasn't the place people went for walks. Miles from anywhere, or anything, it was completely deserted.

Beckett had told her one time that dogs could ascertain the sum of a person's character after one brief encounter. She didn't need more than a glance now to know that this man meant to harm her. Whoever it was, his intent was clear. Catch her. To kill her? Her stomach coiled tight.

Frantically, she scanned ahead. Nothing but a solitary two-lane road. On one side the shoulder flattened out into the endless expanse of dry earth without so much as a bush or a tree for concealment. On the other, more flat acres that eventually rose up to meet the rippling foothills that would be burnished gold in the daylight. At the moment they were inky outlines against a darker sky.

She fought her rising panic. There had to be an escape, but where should she run? She'd been paralleling the road, dialing the phone as she went, but her fingers shook too badly and she had not yet been able to complete the call. Should she stop now and try again? But what about

the man? Compromising, she texted Jude
and Willow as she kept moving.

Kenny at borax works with Beckett. Went
for help. Heading east. Somebody following me. Scared.

Jude would be able to figure out her
general location, but what about Beckett?
Had he been able to overcome Kenny? To
escape?

Kenny's probably armed. He'll kill you.

*…it's going to be the hardest thing he
ever does in his entire miserable life.*

What if Kenny had already succeeded?
And then he'd sent his compatriot to finish
his terrible mission. The thought lodged
in her throat, constricting her windpipe.

Fear began to work its poison, paralyzing her limbs and nibbling away at
her reason. Her body was depleted, exhausted, muscles too tired even to keep up
a brisk walking pace, but still she forced
herself to hurry on along the road. Something warm oozed into the back of her

sock, blood from her heel scraping against her shoe.

Ahead stretched the obsidian sky, washed with stars. No sign of Willow's vehicle or any of the National Park Service personnel who had nightly patrols. Not even a single tourist in search of the ultimate stargazing.

The man crunched along behind her, shoulders erect, unhurried, yet closing the distance between them anyway. Still no sign of any approaching cars.

Figure it out, she commanded herself. Should she make for the foothills, where she might find a place to hide? But they were so distant, and her speed had dropped to little more than a fast hobble. There would be no outrunning her pursuer. Option B? Fight.

Laney was not particularly athletic, nor competitive. Her foster parents had suggested she join the high school basketball team, but while her skills were decent, she had never acquired the thirst for winning like the other girls. Could she actually defend herself physically? A day ago she wouldn't have thought so, but now it was the only way to save her baby's life.

What weapon could she possibly find to aid her on this desolate patch of desert? She patted her pockets with clammy palms. There was nothing in there but a cell phone, and the lighter she always carried and…bug spray. She recalled the directions saying something about avoiding the eye area. Her fingers closed around the slender cylinder.

Was it even good anymore? Had it expired?

But she'd have to let him get close enough, and if it failed…

She swallowed hard. Again she scanned for another idea, any other possible way to escape, evade or at least delay. There was not one ray of hope in the yawning emptiness all around her. Hardly able to draw breath, she took the spray from her pocket and eased the cap off. One try, one chance to save herself and her baby.

Since her speed was already ebbing

away, it was a small adjustment to slow a bit more. Now she could clearly hear him advancing, heavy steps crunching into the soil on the shoulder of the road, his breathing noisy. She let him close the gap even more, sending up a silent plea to the Lord for her and her child. Closer he came. The hair on her neck prickled.

Closer.

Still he hadn't said a word.

She allowed him two more steps before she whirled around, holding the canister chest high. Perhaps he would think it was pepper spray or mace.

The man, she now saw, was heavily bearded, long hair snaking to his shoulders. He was somewhere in the neighborhood of his late sixties, she thought. He did not look startled that she'd spoken, nor interested in the weapon she held. "Who are you?"

"Kenny's uncle, Leonard."

"What do you want?"

"You know." He paused and spit on the ground.

"My husband didn't kill Pauline," she blurted.

He let out a hard laugh. "Course you'd lie for him."

"I'm not lying, and neither is Beckett." She forced steel into her tone.

He went silent then. Goose bumps stood up along her skin.

She kept the spray aimed at him. "What do you intend to do, now that you've caught up with me?"

"Come to fetch you, while Kenny keeps your hubby busy."

She gulped. Kenny's attack at the borax works had been a ruse...so he could carry out his plan. Kill her, then Beckett.

Her blood went icy and she fought the shivers. She tried to keep from clutching the spray trigger too hard and accidentally deploying it.

"You're not taking me anywhere."

He smiled then, no words needed to convey the malice in his heart. There was no warmth, no compassion, nothing in his expression but hatred. Was he close enough? Did she have the nozzle of the spray aimed correctly?

One chance...

He shoved his hands in his pocket and pulled out a cord.

She bit her lip. "You're going to strangle me?"

He shook his head. "Nah. I'm going to take you back to Kenny and let him do it. That's justice. Beckett killed Pauline. Kenny kills you. It's proper."

She swallowed the brick in her throat. "That won't work. I can't walk all the way back. You can't carry me. I'm too heavy."

"True," he said. "Gonna knock you out, tie you up and roll you off the road and out of sight, pile some sand over you, maybe. We'll be back with the car. You'll keep just fine...like a side of beef I got in my deep freeze." He laughed.

"I'll keep running and fighting." She thought of Beckett. "It will be the hardest thing you've ever done."

He grinned. "Like I tell Kenny, difficult things are the most rewarding." He took the final step forward. She squeezed the trigger. The stream of liquid arced out in a silver thread from the nozzle. The spray did not hit him squarely in the eyes as she'd hoped, but it was close enough. He clawed at his face, reeling back, coughing and spluttering. She advanced, kept on spraying until there was nothing left in her canister.

He cried out and collapsed to his knees. She didn't wait any longer, whirling off along the road, sending another text as she went.

Help me.

And then it was pure persistence, one bloody foot in front of the other, in the direction Willow had taken. Each step was agony. "Only a little farther," she whispered to the baby. "We're gonna make it—you'll see."

Surely by now, Willow or Jude had gotten the message and alerted the National Park Service rangers. Help was on the way, for her and Beckett. Her shins ached and the pain in her feet felt like she was walking on razor blades. After a few yards, she risked a look over her shoulder.

Time stood still. Her mind whirled. A sound reflected off the road, a desperate keening moan. It took her a moment to realize it was her own cry, as she watched Uncle Leonard rise to his feet and come after her.

Beckett crested the slope down which he'd tumbled. He wasn't sure if he would be running right into the point of Kenny's knife, but he couldn't wait. Laney's scream rang in his memory and flooded him with adrenaline.

He had to get to the van, to get to her.

There was no sign of Kenny as he plowed through the ruins, stumbling and banging his knees, scrambling up again, tripping, falling, rising, until he finally made it to the entrance point. Below, Kenny's car was still there in the parking lot, lights on, engine running. Beckett didn't take time to puzzle it over. He thundered down the slope, just as Kenny slammed the driver's door.

He fired a mirthless grin at Beckett as he peeled out of the lot in a shower of gravel. The sedan turned left, the direction Laney had taken. Fear punched him squarely in the gut.

He ran to the van and leaped into the driver's seat, cranked the key.

The engine throbbed, coughed and died.

He banged on the steering wheel. "Come on, come on." How many times had they thought about replacing the old vehicle and how many more times had another expense been deemed more important? Beckett's cousin Austin was an excellent mechanic, and he'd kept the old van going with spare parts and sheer persistence.

He cranked the key again. Same result.

He heard Laney's voice from a long-ago memory. "Vannie is sensitive. Be gentle."

"It's a car, Laney."

"So is a Rolls-Royce, but you'd treat that better than Vannie, wouldn't you?"

Her fanciful notions of how to treat a hunk of metal and gears amused him at the time, delighted him, as had most things about his imaginative wife.

Forcing in three calm breaths, he tried once more, turning the key with more delicacy than before. It started up, easy as pie. "Yes," he hollered, pulling the van away from the broken-glass pile on the ground. The rear doors were hopelessly mashed, welded ajar by the impact of Kenny's fender.

He jammed his foot on the gas, stopping abruptly when he heard the beeping of his cell phone. He snatched it up. He had no time to speak before Jude started in.

"We're on our way," Jude said.

"They're after her..."

"I know. I called her back, but she's not answering."

He hit the speaker button and dropped the cell onto the passenger seat.

"Where's Kenny?" Jude asked.

"Heading north after Laney. He had backup. I'm following." He rammed the gas pedal down and the wrecked van surged forward, wind blowing through the open cargo doors.

"Beckett, I'm two minutes from your location. Clouder's got a paramedic responding too. Wait right there."

"This is a satellite phone." He quickly shared his coordinates. "You can track me."

"Wait."

He didn't answer. The phone skidded off the seat as he lurched out onto the road.

"Beckett," Jude shouted.

Beckett rolled out, his headlights scouring the shoulder on each side of the road. He knew she would have kept to the road, her best chance at help. Kenny must be ahead of him by a matter of minutes.

Scared... What had he done allowing Kenny to find them so easily? And then he'd sent Laney off and running, oblivious to the fact that Kenny had brought a cohort.

Dumb move, Beckett. She's smart not to trust you. You led her right into a trap.

A fox darted across the road and he swerved to avoid it. A predator out stalking prey, just like Kenny and his helper. Kenny's smile had been satisfied, as he sped from the borax works. Why hadn't Beckett recognized the diversion?

"Focus," he snarled at himself. Self-recrimination could wait until after he found her.

Found her...but what if he was too late? His petite, pregnant wife, desperate, alone, terrified. She would not last long against two men intent on murdering her.

He slammed that thought down tight and punched the gas. He stared into the darkness for any sign of movement. She had no flashlight except for her cell phone, and that was pretty useless against the vast Death Valley darkness. To escape Kenny's partner, she might have headed for the foothills. Too far, he thought. Too much exposed ground to cover without being seen.

Stopping for a moment, he stuck his head out the open window, listening.

Ahead, a pile of tumbled rocks partially concealed the turn in the road. Was that the throb of an engine? He goosed the gas. The van lurched ahead with a roar. When Beckett cleared the rocks, there on the straightaway was Kenny's damaged sedan.

It was pulled to the side, passenger-side door open, headlights off, engine running. A thick-bodied man was lumbering toward it. Uncle Leonard. No surprise. Where was Laney?

Had they subdued her, gotten her into the sedan with them? Locked her in the trunk? He cranked the van. Fifty yards and closing. There was a loud pop and the van began to buck. The blown tire sent Beckett skidding into a lazy spiral across the road. Sweat beaded his forehead. He turned into the skid and wrestled the car to a stop. In his peripheral vision, he saw Kenny and his uncle leaping into the sedan and slamming the doors.

By the time he brought the van back under control, Kenny was already speeding out of sight. Strobing lights and sirens announced the approach of the NPS or Jude or both from a half mile behind him.

He forced the van back out onto the road, slowly now, ignoring the grinding sound where the tire rim hit the asphalt. Indecision clawed at him. Had they taken her? Or was she hiding someplace nearby? Or... He gulped down the acid taste in his throat.

"Laney," he shouted out the window. There was no answer but the squeal of the damaged tire as he idled along the roadway. Leaving the engine running, he grabbed a flashlight from the van and stalked along the roadway, light scanning for any telling signs.

The light shook in his hand as he saw the disturbed dirt, puckered into trails. Had she been dragged? He shouted again, his cry a minuscule blip in the wide-open space.

No sign of her.

Desperation crawled up his spine, digging claws into his stomach. They must have her, and he'd let them get away. He had to follow, as best as he could, for as long as the van could still move.

He leaped back inside and his foot hit the gas. He was flying after them, futility making him shout aloud. "This isn't going to happen," he hollered into the inky night air, the breeze snatching away his desperation. Laney would often tell him that God wanted to hear the sorrow as well as the celebration.

Right now, he thought he would be swallowed up by the yawning fear inside. When he thought the feeling would cause him to explode, he shouted the words. "Lord, help me. I can't find her."

Again, the night greeted him only with emptiness. The sirens were closer now and he plowed on, not knowing what else to do. A figure hunched next to the road not ten feet ahead of him. One pale hand outthrust to shield her eyes from the glare of his headlights. He nearly stood on the brakes, the squeal of tires sickening. He exploded from the car.

"Beckett?" The word was so soft and weak, he almost didn't hear it. His heart surged full force against his ribs as he grabbed her up. The relief was a trail of silver light that filled him from toes to the top of his head. It was several seconds before he could breathe.

She sobbed in his arms, tears wetting his shirt. "They were going to kill me. They heard you coming and I ran. They would have killed me, Beckett." She was wobbly, trembling. "They would have killed our baby."

Her legs shook and he scooped her up, carried her to the passenger seat of the still-running van. For a few moments he simply held her, as tight as he dared, showing her with his touch that she was safe.

Her shuddering cries took over and left her unable to speak.

He stroked her shoulders, touched her hair, cradled her close. "It's okay, honey. I've got you now. They're gone."

They weren't gone, not really, but at the

moment he would have sawed himself in half if it would have comforted her. He pulled a blanket around her and held her to his chest while she cried.

"Cops are right behind us. We'll get you to a hospital."

"They'll come," she cried. "They'll find me."

"No," he said, holding her face and urging her to look at him. "They are gone. You are safe."

For now. The words seemed to help, and she gulped in a steadying breath while he pulled the blanket tighter around her shoulders. Kenny and good old Uncle Leonard were still out there, probably celebrating how close they'd gotten to making good on their threat. One enemy had morphed into two.

As he held Laney close and reassured her as best he could, the National Park Service vehicle careened into view.

Go ahead and celebrate, Kenny, he thought grimly. *It'll be time for you to pay up soon enough*. He would make sure that they were locked up if it was the last thing he did on this planet. They would never touch Laney or the baby ever again.

ELEVEN

Laney opened her eyes to a startling brightness. A creamy wall held a whiteboard with strange notations and check marks next to a name, her name, Duke, Laney. There were numbers there, and marks and initials, some kind of checklist. A medicinal scent tickled her nostrils. She blinked hard, trying to place herself in space and time. Her head pounded and muscles ached everywhere, as if she'd been put through the tumble cycle of the dryer.

A calloused hand covered hers. Beckett stood over her, haggard, a hole in his T-shirt and a shadow of stubble on his chin. Why hadn't he shaved? Memories trickled in from a nightmare, running, terror, faceless strangers pursuing. No, not a nightmare, she realized. She bolted upright, a scream on her lips.

"It's okay," Beckett said. "You're safe. The NPS had you flown to a Las Vegas hospital."

"Hospital? The baby..." she croaked, hands flying to her stomach, noting the IV taped to her hand. Why couldn't she remember what had happened?

"Muffin is fine. You are too." He flashed her a tenuous smile. "Minor cuts and bruises and mild dehydration. They were worried about shock and the pregnancy. Just precautionary to transport you here."

Precautionary... She relaxed a notch. Still, she touched the swell of her tummy, just to reassure herself. "Kenny's uncle came after me. I sprayed him with insect repellent."

Beckett's smile kindled some light in his eyes. "I know. Couldn't be prouder."

She squirmed, feeling her cheeks pinken. She wished he would not look at her quite so closely, but he was outright staring, and there was nowhere for her to hide unless she pulled the covers over her face.

He held a cup with a straw to her mouth. "How about some water? Hydrating, remember?"

She sipped gratefully to ease the dryness in her throat. As much as she was fearful to know the answer, she asked anyway. "Did they catch...?"

"No." His mouth firmed into a line. "Kenny and his uncle are still at large, but they won't be for long. Jude's going to meet with us when you're back home."

Still at large. The bottom dropped out of her stomach. She wriggled her toes. As much as she felt careworn and tattered, the thought of lying in a hospital bed evoked downright helplessness in her spirit. "When can I get out of here?"

He smiled. "Maybe in a couple of hours." His cell phone rang. He answered and covered the phone. "It's Dr. Irene. I called her when we got here. Probably woke her up, but the doctors were giving me so much information and I couldn't understand it all. Are you up to speaking with her?"

Laney nodded and he put the phone on Speaker.

"Laney, I've spoken to your doctor," Irene said, without preamble. "Like I told Beckett, everything is fine. Baby's heartbeat is strong, and your blood pressure is perfect too. Both of you are going to be okay, do you understand?"

Laney laughed. "Yes, ma'am, but why do you sound like a medical drill sergeant?"

There was a long sigh and then her tone gentled. "Sorry. I was just so worried when Beckett called. He was freaking out."

Beckett grimaced. "I wouldn't say freaking out. Maybe highly concerned."

Irene ignored his comment. There was a little break in her voice when she spoke. "You are not only my patient, Laney— you're the first friend I ever had in this town."

Laney's heart warmed. Irene had moved from a big city and found the ponderous quiet and minimal people contact hard to adjust to. Not like Laney, who had immediately embraced the desert culture, from the ferocious heat of the summer, when travelers were nonexistent, to the cooler autumns, which brought the gush of tourists that would sustain them through the inhospitable seasons. But Death Valley was an acquired taste for some people, including Irene. She was constantly in a state of motion, as opposed to the natives, who paced themselves. Judging from the collection of travel and fashion magazines in Irene's waiting room, she might be still making that adjustment.

"I'm okay, like you said. Sore all over, but ready to go home."

"What can I do from here? I offered to come to Las Vegas, but Beckett said you might be returning home today anyhow. How can I help in the meantime?"

"Can you please go and make sure Herm is taking care of Admiral? He does a pretty good job, but he'll have his hands full running things without Beckett and me, and he might forget about my poor old doggy. Admiral will sleep until dinnertime if he's allowed to."

She laughed. "Smart dog. Of course I will. I was there at the hotel, after my run, when Beckett called me. The guests were talking about what happened. Willow said she didn't get your text in time. She feels terrible."

"It's okay. Beckett found me." She pressed down a shiver as the memory swam in: Beckett arriving by the narrowest of margins, to scare off Leonard and Kenny. Five minutes later and where would she have wound up? "I'm sorry the guests were upset."

Beckett leaned closer to the phone. Laney noticed a series of scratches and scrapes fanning out along his neck. What had happened between him and Kenny after she ran for help? The memory of the vast darkness and the terror it concealed made her pulse skitter.

"I'm sorry I called you so early, Doc," Beckett said into the phone. "I appreciate your help to understand all those test results the doctor was throwing out."

Again, the unexpected note of humility in his voice caught her attention as he continued.

"You said you saw the guests this morning?"

"Yes. They were in the breakfast room when I stopped for coffee."

Beckett frowned. "Who exactly?"

"A family and two teen boys who looked bored out of their gourds. Willow was there too."

"And Rita Brown?"

"Who?"

"A guest." He paused. "Long hair in a braid whenever I've seen her. She's staying in 205."

"I didn't see anyone like that. Why do you ask about her?"

"She says she's a journalist, doing a story on me. She's from the same town as Pauline."

They could hear Irene's gasp. "That cannot be a coincidence, can it? What's going on?"

"I don't know. She asked to stay in Pauline's room."

There was silence on the other end of the phone. "From Pauline's town and staying in the same room? Why?"

"We don't know," Laney put in, "but be careful, okay? Tell us if you hear anything."

Irene agreed. "Let's move up our Monday appointment to Saturday. That will ease your mind, won't it?"

Laney nodded, relief so strong it felt like a warm blanket.

Irene ended the call with promises to check on Admiral and give him a snack.

After they disconnected, Laney breathed slowly, trying to take inventory of the aches and pains. She settled deeper into the pillows, wishing the pounding behind her temples would ease.

Beckett walked around the room, distracted and brooding.

"How did you get here?" she asked suddenly. "To Las Vegas, I mean."

"Levi took me back to the hotel to get my truck and I drove here. Would have just taken the van. It's still drivable, but I didn't want to take the time to change the tire."

"And you stayed here all night?"

He nodded.

"No wonder you look exhausted. Have you eaten?"

A slight smile curved his mouth. "Aren't you the one in the hospital bed?"

She scanned the sheets tucked neatly around her. "I don't even remember being admitted, or the helicopter ride or anything."

"You were...real upset. I think maybe you don't want to remember it. I tried to go in the helicopter with you, but they don't allow it. I did everything I could to convince the flight nurse." His gaze drifted down to her stomach and a look of pain tightened his features.

"What is it?" she said.

"Nothing."

"It's something."

"Naw," he said. "Nothing worth talking about."

An ache behind her temples flared up. Suddenly it all seemed too wearying and her patience thinned to the breaking point. "Haven't we been through enough that you don't have to put on the tough-guy persona?"

He stared, surprised. "I'm not. You're in the hospital."

He seemed to feel this was adequate explanation. She rolled her eyes. "That is a fact—I am indeed in the hospital, so I've got plenty of time to hear how you're feeling."

"You don't need to be burdened."

She straightened on the pillow. "Beckett," she said, "stop trying to decide what I need. We were partners once, and even then you kept things from me."

He looked dumbfounded. "What things?"

"Your feelings."

He quirked a brow. "But those aren't worth anything."

She would have pinched his ear if she could have reached. "Those are worth everything," she managed to say without raising her voice or adding *you dolt*.

He raised his palms. "I don't know what you want me to say. What have I kept from you?"

"Why didn't you tell me you were meeting Pauline the day she was killed?" The question appeared to have surprised him as much as it had her. Why had she aired it? Why now? "You said you didn't want to wake me, but that wasn't all of it."

He was silent for a moment. "I don't see why it's important anymore."

She folded her arms and stared him down until the silence became like a live thing between them.

He cleared his throat. "She was acting odd, urgent, like she had something life-and-death to tell me. But she was always one of those dramatic types, so the note she left fit right in. She'd...uh...contacted me once or twice a while back after her divorce, before you and I got together."

She knew him well enough to wait out the pause.

"Laney..." He pulled in a breath. "Our life was good, perfect, and everything from my high school days ended so badly. I didn't want any part of that to touch what we had. I was going to tell her I couldn't help her, to ask her to leave...but she was already dead."

"You should have told me before you met her."

"Yes, I should. Like I said, she was from a time when I was...someone else, who wasn't worth much."

"Beckett... There aren't two of you. What you've been through made you who you are."

He was quiet. "I don't know what to say."

"You hurt someone, accidentally. You aren't a monster."

"That's what the town called me then. They still do."

"You let them tell you who you were." The regret in his eyes almost stopped her breath. "God doesn't condemn you for what happened in high school, Beckett. Don't you think you should follow His lead?"

"It's too late. I wrecked what we had too. I ruined us."

She forced herself to look at him. "Yes, you did, but you're a free man. You still have a life to live."

His voice came from far away, a murmur of profound pain. "Not anymore. Everything good in my life is right here in this bed. All I can do is to make sure you and the baby are going to be okay."

It seemed unbearable to witness his grief for one moment longer. She reached out her hand and took his, but he would not meet her eye.

What could she say? He'd been so careful to hide this brokenness from her, trying desperately to reinvent an identity that was separate from the monstrous one he'd taken to heart. If only he'd shared his vulnerability sooner, maybe things would have been different. Maybe he would never have walked into those woods alone that day. It was almost too painful to consider. She squeezed his hand, and she felt some of her long-burning anger ebb away. She knew now why their marriage had really died. How could a man truly love her when he hated himself?

Beckett was grateful that Jude rapped a knuckle on the hospital room door and stuck his head in. The conversation was reaching the point of intolerability. Trent Clouder in a fire-department T-shirt followed Jude into the room, carrying a bunch of yellow carnations.

"The volunteers wanted you to have some flowers," Clouder said.

"Thank you so much, but I hope you didn't drive all the way from Furnace Falls to bring me flowers."

He shrugged. "I was on scene with the ambulance. When we got the details of what had happened and who the victim was..." He shook his head. "Well, it just about blew my mind. When Pauline was in town, she mentioned her brother, just said he was in and out of trouble, but she adored him. Never figured she meant he was that out of control."

Beckett wondered exactly how much time the two had spent together for that kind of information to come out. Jude beat him to the question.

"So you spoke to her when she came back to Furnace Falls?" Jude asked.

He nodded. "Couple days before she was murdered."

Beckett flinched.

Jude hooked his thumbs on his belt. "You didn't mention it before."

And he hadn't elaborated much with Beckett either.

Trent shrugged. "Not a lot to say. We had coffee. She told me she was staying at the Hotsprings. I gave her my number and told her I'd like to take her out to dinner while she was in town, but...well, we never got the chance."

"Did she seem upset?" Jude asked. "Preoccupied with something?"'

"No, more excited, I'd say. She didn't mention anything specific."

Jude cocked his head. "I'm still trying to digest what you're saying. You didn't come forward to tell us any of this after her body was found."

Trent's cheeks went dusky. "I was trying to keep my marriage together. My wife was threatening divorce, and I didn't want to give her any more ammo, you know?"

Ammo, like asking another woman out for dinner? Beckett tried to keep his feelings from showing.

"Anyway, it was just that one conversation over coffee, so I didn't think it would have been particularly helpful."

"How did Kenny know where we were?" Laney said.

"Herm," Beckett said. "He told me a guy called the hotel asking about a starlight tour. Herm filled him in on the details without thinking, our usual stops, etc. After he hung up, Herm got to thinking he'd made a mistake and called me at the borax works. Kenny was able to put together where we were, but I still wonder if he had some inside help. Maybe from Rita?"

"Rita? Your hotel guest?" Clouder's expression was alive with curiosity. "The one asking the librarian about you?"

"Actually," Jude said, "I need to talk to Laney right now and get my facts straight. Would you mind stepping out, Trent?"

"No problem. I was leaving anyway." He laid the bouquet on the table. "Everyone will be thrilled to know you and the baby are okay." He kissed her cheek before he left the room.

Beckett felt a prickle of annoyance. A kiss? And how had Trent known about Laney's pregnancy?

He could tell by the look on his cousin's face that Jude was also pondering that question.

"Laney," Jude said, "I'm sorry, but I've got to ask you to tell me everything you remember about what happened from the time you left the borax works."

Beckett's gut squeezed at the look of fear that trickled across Laney's delicate features. His rage that Kenny had terrorized her, hunted her like an animal, made it hard for him to breathe.

"She needs rest, Jude. Can't it wait?"

Jude turned a gaze on him that was not completely without warmth. "You know it can't," he said calmly. "So you stay in here and remain silent, or you step out in the hallway, but either way, you don't interrupt. Got me?"

Beckett swallowed. He knew his cousin was right. "All right," he said, taking a seat in the hard-backed chair, steeling himself as Laney began to relive the nightmare all over again.

TWELVE

Laney had not thought she could produce so many tears, but relating the facts to Jude unleashed torrents of them that subsided into shuddering gasps. True to his word, Beckett did not speak, but he rose from his chair. The feel of his work-toughened hands, caressing her fingers, transferred some strength to her, and she was able to make it through.

Jude closed his notebook. "You did real well, Laney. Couldn't ask for more. I've got to go now, but I can tell you, once Mom hears about this, she's going to camp out on your doorstep with soup and cookies."

Laney giggled and wiped her eyes. "Admiral and I will be thrilled to partake of

Aunt Kitty's cookies, especially if they're the walnut-and-date kind."

"Oh, they will be," he said. "And I'll get her a fresh box of dates from Duff's farm to seal the deal."

"Those are the best dates in the world," Laney said. The guests at the Hotsprings Hotel usually concurred after they toured the little family-run farm.

"Uh-huh. Whenever I pick them up, I get chapter and verse on that from Duff. I'll see you soon."

Beckett walked Jude to the door, their voices too low for her to hear. She caught only Beckett's heartfelt, "Thank you, Jude. I mean, thanks for coming yourself instead of sending someone."

"Family," Jude said.

Family. Did he mean the word to encompass his cousin again? Or just her, his pseudo sister? She wondered if perhaps Jude and Beckett would be able to bridge the chasm of their distrust and become proper cousins again. Jude left and Beckett retreated into silence as the nurse came in to check her vitals.

She wanted to spiral back to their earlier conversation.

Everything good in my life is right here in this bed. All I can do is to make sure you and the baby are going to be okay.

She had the sensation of urgency, that the fragile thread that now connected them would snap as soon as they left the surreal environment of the hospital. "Beckett..." she started.

A brisk knock robbed her of the chance. The doctor arrived. Beckett stepped away, shoving his big hands in his pockets.

"Good morning," the doctor said to Laney. "Glad to see you're awake. I've already spoken to your husband."

Husband. The word had filled her with pride once upon a time. Now it echoed with uncertainty. How much longer would they be married? As soon as Kenny was caught, Beckett would leave as promised. It was the best choice for everyone. She swallowed a sudden lump in her throat.

The doctor washed his hands and pulled on a pair of rubber gloves. "Long story short, the baby is fine and so are you. If everything continues to look good, we'll get you out of here in the late afternoon."

She'd known he would say that, but still the breath whooshed out of her. "Music to my ears."

"Oh, I think we can do better than that," he said, applying warm gel to an ultrasound wand. "I'm going to do a fetal Doppler test." He cocked an amused eye at Beckett.

"Ready, Mr. Duke?"

Beckett looked startled. "Ready for what?"

The doctor laughed and placed the wand against her belly. She closed her eyes and listened to the soft rhythmic whoosh and purr. It was indeed sweeter than music, more delicate than one of the fragile cactus blossoms that would unfurl only for the briefest of moments. Whatever she'd had to endure, the fright she'd felt at her harrowing confrontation, it was all worth it to be able to hear that tiny heartbeat.

Thank You, Lord.

When she opened her eyes, Beckett was standing electrified at the foot of her bed. "Is that...?"

The doctor nodded. "Your baby's heartbeat, Mr. Duke, strong and steady as it should be at four months gestation."

All the color drained from Beckett's cheeks, and then flooded back in again until he was positively pink. He stood there, mouth open and gasping like a fish. "I...uh..."

He stepped backward so quickly he bumped into the table and sent a plastic pitcher of water toppling to the floor. Water splashed all over Beckett's shoes and the doctor's pant leg. He looked at his wet boots and then at the doctor and then at her, before his eyes once again locked on the machine still emitting the sounds of the fetal heartbeat.

"Sorry, Doctor. I'll...go get some paper towels to clean this up." And before the doctor could say a word, he'd bolted out the door, ignoring the paper-towel dispenser on the wall not two feet away.

She gaped. "Did he just run out?"

The doctor smiled. "Like a startled rabbit. You can never predict how the reality of parenthood will affect a fellow. Believe me, I've seen reactions I can't even describe, but he won't go far, I can promise you that."

"How do you know?"

The doctor stripped off his gloves. "Not to put too fine a point on it, but your husband has been a pain in my side since we admitted you."

She stared. "Uh-oh. What has he done?"

"It's more what he wouldn't do. He refused to budge from the examining room. He was what my mama would call *het up*. I had to call Security before he would consent to banish himself to the hallway outside while we finished our examination. There's no chair right outside the door and the waiting room was just too far away for his taste, so he stood there, like some sort of stone monument, only not as quiet. Every time someone would enter or exit he would politely harangue them about your condition until the nurses were ready to personally pitch him out the front door. I relented and let him enter the room if he would promise not to say a word. Figured it would be more productive than having him hauled off by the cops."

"Thank you for that, Doctor."

"Yes, ma'am. He kept his promise and stopped badgering the nurses and let them do their jobs, so he was allowed to stay. He's a big guy, but he mashed himself into the corner so as not to get in their way."

She sank back on the pillow. "I can't believe it." But actually, she could. When they'd been married only a few weeks, she'd gotten such a bad case of the flu that she wanted him to sleep in an empty tent so as not to catch it. He'd refused, bringing her ice chips and sips of water and finally jaggedly cut squares of half-burnt dry toast he'd insisted on making himself instead of asking Herm. She'd secretly fed a few to Admiral on the sly.

But why had he run out of the room when he'd heard their baby's heartbeat?

The doctor seemed to read her mind. "New life is powerful, isn't it? It gives us a fresh way to see the world." He smiled once more. "I'll get your discharge papers ready, Mrs. Duke. Take good care of yourself."

A fresh way to see the world. An idea ignited in her heart. Could this baby be a way for Beckett to see the world, and himself, the way God meant? The spark warmed her imagination. If he could make that monumental shift...might it be possible that they could start life anew? Together?

No, she told herself. He was here only long enough to deal with Kenny Sanderson. He'd asked for a divorce, refused to even speak to her throughout the months of his incarceration. He'd not loved her enough to journey through the "worse" part of "for better or worse" with her. He'd walked away, like her foster parents had, and a baby wasn't going to change that. She didn't love him anyway, not anymore.

But in a very tiny whisper, she said, "God, please put his heart back together again. He needs You."

She sank into an exhausted sleep.

Beckett was grateful that Laney dozed in the truck as he drove them toward Death Valley. Jude had arranged for a Las Vegas cop to follow them out of the city until an Inyo County officer took over as they drew closer to home. He was grateful for the police protection, appreciative of Jude's proactiveness. As the miles wound by, he kept stealing glances at her, the sound of the baby's heartbeat pinging in his memory.

He made sure the air-conditioning vents were not blowing directly on her and turned off the radio sports channel that he was regularly tuned in to. Should he wake her and insist she sip from the water bottle in her cup holder? The doctor had said hydration was important...but wasn't sleep important too? He smiled, recalling the whoosh of the baby's heartbeat.

Something, he recognized, had happened to him when he'd heard that heartbeat. It was as if the small pattering had echoed through his whole being and set his own heart thunking in a whole new rhythm. What had happened, he could not exactly articulate. He'd known perfectly well there was an infant growing inside Laney, but now everything felt different. The baby, their baby, was a tiny person, a living human in perfect miniature.

He'd gone on his phone, while Laney had slept in the hospital bed, and done some research. The site he visited said that at the fourth month of gestation, the baby would have fingers and toes, even a downy coating of hair, maybe.

Surely it would, since Laney's hair was a glorious thick crown and he had to shave regularly to avoid a five-o'clock shadow. It was only natural that their baby would have a wonderful head of... He blinked hard. What was the matter with him? Imagining what their baby's attributes might be? Hadn't he promised he was going to step out of this child's life? But he'd learned that the baby could even now be sucking its thumb, deep in its watery world. His cousin Willow had sucked her thumb until she was well on to five. But that might be a problem, he realized, because it could cause the need for braces, as it had for Willow. With a mental smack, he brought himself to heel.

Stop it. You have to leave.

That thought stabbed a pain deep into his core. Could he really walk away from Laney and his baby? To reduce his contact to child-support payments and letters, an occasional visit or phone call if Laney would allow it? A thought flowed out, one that had bloomed unbidden in his mind the moment he'd heard the pulse of his baby's heart. If Jude could capture Kenny... maybe then... But he did not allow himself to complete the thought. Danger or not, he'd broken her heart and her trust.

No good, came the remembered echoes of the townspeople. Monster.

He dragged a look to Laney again. The baby would have half of his genes, wouldn't it? What if...? If Muffin had Laney for a mother, the baby would be just fine, even if they did have a fair share of his DNA.

He remembered something his father used to say. *God don't make junk.* The fragile heartbeat he'd eavesdropped upon made him agree. There was nothing about that tiny life growing in there but pure, 100 percent God-in-action. The thought startled him.

A beautiful ache spiraled through him, tumbling and slow like he imagined the baby was, floating in Laney's belly, sucking a miniature thumb. In the silence of his heart, he thanked God. It was the first time in a very long time he'd humbled himself so completely. *Thank You*, he said silently, *that I got to hear those precious beats*. He didn't deserve it, but he'd take it and hold it close for the remainder of his days.

Laney stirred once they rolled into the valley, straightening with a wince.

"Pain?"

"Headache," she groaned, pressing her palms to her temples.

"I'll call Dr. Irene and ask what you can take for it."

"I already know what I can take for it." Her chin went up. "A chocolate milkshake with whipped cream and three cherries."

He stared for a moment before the laughter burst out of him. "A milkshake? That's what you and Muffin need?"

"Yes." She nodded solemnly. "No peanuts, though. Muffin doesn't like them." She kept a completely straight face except for the barest hint of mischief.

He managed the question around his wide grin. "How do you know Muffin doesn't like peanuts?"

"We get heartburn."

"Ah. Well, I'm sure we can meet those requirements." He flat out marveled at her ability to think about ice cream and joke after what she'd experienced in the last twenty-four hours. Whoever said women were the weaker gender had obviously not known any very well.

She sat back with a sigh, a dreamy look on her face, perhaps contemplating her dessert.

Excitement prickled his nerves. He could hardly conceive of it. Was he being allowed to participate in soothing one of those pregnancy craving things? The thought delighted him so much, he drove quickly to an ice-cream shop before the mysterious craving might vanish and she'd change her mind.

He made sure the deputy behind them pulled up close as he explained his ice-cream mission. The cop smiled.

"That's not too bad. When my wife was expecting our second, she made me get sauerkraut, cases of it, day and night. I can't stand the stuff." He declined Beckett's offer to buy him a shake, as well. He hurried inside to complete the purchase.

The smile…that lovely radiant grin when he handed her the milkshake twirled through him like a runaway dust storm. He was transported back to the joy he'd felt when she'd accepted his proposal, the days when the world was a beautiful place.

Laney was admiring the sweet concoction. "You got the three cherries too. Muffin and I thank you." She set about consuming it with gusto until the last sip was gone.

"Headache better?"

"Much," she said.

He'd helped. He'd eased her pain. His elation lasted until they drew up to the Hotsprings Hotel and Willow came sprinting out. She helped Laney out of the car and threw her arms around her. "I am so sorry. I didn't see your text. You could have died." Two tears rolled down her freckled cheeks.

"She needs to lie down," he said, to forestall the emotional storm he knew was coming from his impetuous cousin, but Laney was already striding toward the dining room. He managed to get ahead of her to open up the door, but Herm was there. He clasped her to his narrow chest. He didn't speak a word, just squeezed her to him until she kissed his cheek.

"I shouldn't have blabbed to Kenny on the phone," Herm said. "I think my brain must be getting old. I..."

"I'm all right," she said. "And you did nothing wrong. How have you been holding up?" And then they were all following her like a row of ducklings while she surveyed the kitchen. Dinner preparations were already in process, the small kettle boiling a supply of potatoes for mashing and a single pan of pork chops in the oven. Laney peeked in and frowned.

"Why so few chops?"

Herm looked cowed. "Well, you see, uh..."

"The Timmons family checked out early," Willow said.

"Yeah," Herm said. "They were sort of upset at what happened to you. Rita's still here, though, and another family of four are supposed to be checking in in a couple of days."

Laney looked crestfallen. "So Rita is our only guest?"

"Uh-huh." Herm shrugged. "Can't figure on why she'd want to stay, though. She isn't signed up for any tours or stuff, and she don't seem to like my cooking. Jude is with her now."

Beckett spun on his heel.

Laney stopped him with a hand on his arm. "Wait, Beckett. Jude won't want you interfering."

"If she tipped Kenny off, I have the right to interfere."

Still she held on. "Since there's no need for a full dinner service, I'm going to go take a shower and sit with Admiral for a while. Will you walk me?"

And because there was nothing in the world which he would not do to keep Laney safe, he nodded and followed her out. Aunt Kitty, Jude's mother and Laney's adopted mother, stepped out of the cabin first, holding Admiral. The dog wriggled and squirmed until she put him down. Laney scooped him up and cuddled and cooed over him before she hugged Aunt Kitty.

Kitty was a full foot shorter than Laney, a full foot shorter than practically anyone. Her silver-black head of tightly curled hair barely made it to midchest on him. There were no square angles on the woman. She was "well insulated," as she liked to tell people. Kitty had never treated him as a suspect, nor a would-be criminal. She was the same generous soul she'd been since he was a little kid who'd needed his knee bandaged or his button sewn on. Kitty was a mother to scores of people in Furnace Falls even though Kitty herself was the victim of a bad marriage, and her own daughter, Jude's sister, had left town when she was eighteen. Kitty and Jude had not heard a word from her in all those years. Even so, Kitty had a smile for anyone and a heart for everyone. He bent to kiss her.

She kissed him and thumbed his cheek. "You need a shave, honey."

"Yes, ma'am."

She waited until Laney sat in the worn upholstered rocker and Admiral heaved himself into her lap. "Herm was busy, so I put clean sheets on the bed, brought you some cookies and soup too."

"Thank you, Aunt Kitty," Laney said. "You shouldn't have gone to that trouble."

Aunt Kitty endured a painful foot condition, which probably explained why her mouth was pinched with discomfort. She waved them off and shoved her hands into the pockets of her blouse. "Who can't slap on some clean linens? Oh, I almost forgot." She drew an object out. "On my way back from the laundry room, I found this on the ground. Figured you might need it."

Beckett held out his hand.

She dropped a sturdy metal screw in his palm.

"Where exactly did you find it?" he asked.

"On the sidewalk along the two hundreds."

The western wing of the complex. *Room*

205, he thought. He looked closer at the screw.

"Does something need fixing?" Laney said.

He offered a careless nod. "Nothing to worry about. I'll take care of it."

She didn't press him further. He noticed her wince again, as if the headache was back.

"Maybe you should lie down," he suggested.

"I've had plenty of lying down. I want to cuddle with Admiral for a while." She began to croon baby talk to him about smoochies and other inexplicable things.

"I'll go warm up that soup," Aunt Kitty said. "Let me have that sweater too, and I'll pop it in the washer. We'll have a nice chat." She shot a glance at Beckett. "Unless I'm interrupting family time." Her look was hopeful. He knew that she'd probably been praying nonstop for the mending of his marriage.

Could it be possible? God had provided them with a child when they'd thought it was impossible. Was there any way He would allow Beckett to fix what he'd ruined?

Right now, he had other priorities, he reminded himself. She was not safe, not with Kenny and Uncle Leonard at large and Rita in their midst. He studied the screw in his palm.

He had a feeling he knew exactly which room it had come from, but he'd do his homework, just to be sure. There would be no margin for a careless error on his part.

Time to do some fixing.

THIRTEEN

Laney tried to relax into the conversation as she sipped the soup with Aunt Kitty. It was still warm in the early evening, but the air conditioner kept pace. Something niggled at her, a suspicious gleam in Beckett's eye as he looked at the screw Aunt Kitty found.

"You know what, Aunt Kitty?" she said abruptly. "I really need to walk around for a few minutes. I forgot to light the tiki torches. Would you like to have a stroll?"

"Pregnant ladies always get what they want," she said with a smile. "But I might not make it too far since my foot is yammering at me. Silly plantar fasciitis. We can put a man on the moon, but no doctor in the universe can make a shoe insert to ease these old feet."

Laney smiled. "How about just across the courtyard?"

Aunt Kitty offered her elbow. "Milady?"

Admiral waddled along after them as they traveled the flagstone path. The temperature was slipping down into the seventies, a perfect fall evening. She took the lighter she'd rescued from her sweater pocket and set it to the wick of the two tiki torches on either side of the lodge's rear entrance. The grounds were empty, and so was the pool. It pained her to see it. Fall should be their busiest season, with plenty of tourists sitting by the firepits, swimming and riding bikes. Across the fence Levi waved as he tended the horses. The lack of guests at the Hotsprings Hotel was no doubt affecting Levi's business, as well. She hoped he could pick up some other tour groups to make up the slack.

Aunt Kitty walked fairly smoothly until they passed between the lodge and the west wing. Then she winced in pain. Laney regretted encouraging her to walk.

"I'm sorry," she said. "Sit here and rest."

Kitty lowered herself into one of the Adirondack chairs. "Just for a while. Let's enjoy the breeze."

Laney peered along the walkway that edged the west rooms and noticed Beckett knocking on Rita's door.

"I'll just be a minute, okay?"

Kitty smiled. "You know where to find me and my aged feet."

Laney reached Beckett as he knuckled the door of Room 205.

He cocked his head, ready to scold her. "Wave to Aunt Kitty," Laney said. "She's keeping a watchful eye on both of us."

Beckett offered a wave. "Go back and sit with her."

She smiled sweetly. "I think you meant, *Laney, my dear. It's such a pleasant night. Wouldn't you be more comfortable sitting in the company of Aunt Kitty?*"

Before he could reply, Rita's door swung open.

She looked a bit rough, Laney thought. Her normally braided hair was loose and hung about her face in limp waves. She had on the same clothes she'd been wearing at the Death Valley outing.

Rita's look darted from Beckett to Laney. "Are you all right? I felt terrible about what happened."

Beckett started to answer, but Laney spoke first. "I'm all right. Thank you. I'm sorry the tour ended with such drama."

"But you got away from Kenny. That's the important thing. He's dangerous."

"That's an understatement," Beckett said. Rita did not meet his eye.

Laney noticed her tote bag on the floor, bulging with contents. "Are you leaving?"

She looked at the bag as if she hadn't seen it. "Yeah.Tomorrow."

"I'm sorry to hear it."

She shrugged. "It's…a little more dangerous than I imagined. I've…changed my plans."

"Did you find what you were looking for?" Beckett asked.

Her eyes widened. "What do you mean?"

He held up the screw. "I bolted all the wardrobe cabinets into the wall myself, in case of earthquakes. This one is from your room. I checked all the other rooms already."

"Well, I guess it fell out of the wall. Feel free to screw it back in, if it makes you feel better."

"It didn't fall out of the wall of its own accord." He looked over her shoulder. "You were tugging on it, searching for something behind it, weren't you? Maybe something you thought Pauline hid in the room before she was killed?"

Laney could not hide her own surprise. Pauline had hidden something? For one wild moment, her heart leaped. Could it have been evidence that might shed some light on who really murdered her? "Did you find something?"

Rita went still. "No."

"Quit lying," Beckett snarled. "I've got a guy hunting my wife because he thinks I killed his sister."

"I know what kind of man he is." Rita's throat convulsed as she swallowed. "I talked to him."

"What?" she and Beckett cried at once.

"When I first came here, I left a note on his uncle's doorstep with my number. He called me a couple of days ago."

Beckett's body went taut as wire. She could feel the heat emanating off him in angry waves. "Why didn't you tell us? Or a cop? Anyone?"

"I decided I didn't want to be involved with him."

Beckett seemed to be speechless, so Laney stepped in. "What did you say to Kenny?"

"I tried to ask him if he knew who Pauline came here to meet."

"How did you know she'd come here to meet someone?" Beckett said.

Rita appeared not to have heard the question. She chewed her lower lip for a moment. "At first Kenny thought I was working for the cops, and then he accused me of being a friend of yours. He wouldn't listen to anything I had to say. In fact, he was getting around to threatening me when my phone went dead. When I heard what happened to you while we were on a photo tour, how he tracked you to the borax works..." She shivered. "This is all getting out of hand. I thought I wanted to be a big-shot reporter, but I've changed my mind. I'm going back to town meetings and flower shows. I've learned my lesson."

She tried to close the door.

Beckett stopped it with his palm. "You have to tell us, please. What do you know about Pauline? What did you find that made you come here in the first place?"

Rita's phone rang. She answered it, eyes widening before she hung up a few seconds later. "It was Kenny," she said, cheeks gone pale as moonlight. "He said he's going to kill me too if I stick around. I'm leaving in the morning. I dropped my car at the shop because it was overheating. It will be ready by ten and then I'm gone."

"But what did you find?" Laney pleaded,

worried that Beckett would lose it completely.

Rita shook her head. "As soon as I'm clear of this town, I'll call you."

"And tell us what?" Beckett demanded. "This isn't fair."

Laney kept her voice soft and calm. "You're scared. Tell us now. We can get the police to help you, protect you."

Rita jammed her fists to her hips. "If I go to the police, Kenny will know. He's got friends in this town. He will track me down. No, I'm handing this all over to you and you can straighten it out with Kenny. That's all I'm saying. If you send the police here tonight, I won't ever tell you what I have from Pauline."

Then she slammed the door in their faces.

Laney and Beckett walked away a few paces, facing each other in the failing sunlight. When she spoke, Laney was surprised at her eagerness. She took him by the forearms. "Beckett, this might finally be over. She knows something about what happened."

He looked down where her fingers circled his wrists. "I can't really believe it."

"I can. I've been praying for it on my knees every night."

He tilted his head. "You have? Even after I filed for divorce?"

She shrugged. "You don't deserve to be imprisoned. You're innocent."

He was quiet a moment. "And you've always believed in me, haven't you? Even when everyone else was ready to hang me from the highest tree, my cousin Jude included."

She sighed. "They don't know you like I do."

He lifted a hand and stroked her cheek with one finger.

"You were always the best thing that ever happened to me." Before she knew what was happening, he'd leaned down and kissed her. The connection was so sweet, like she'd remembered, only different. He was the one person on the planet who knew her, deeply and completely, and she'd thought she'd known him too.

But he'd asked for a divorce. That betrayal stung her afresh. Hurt rose to overtake the other rush of feeling and she stepped away.

He looked dazed, staring at her with warmth she could not ignore.

"I want you to have your life back, Beckett." She cleared her throat and added, "So you can start fresh."

"Laney…" He stopped and looked at his feet. "Thanks, for believing in me, I mean."

Her throat felt too raw to speak, so she started back to Aunt Kitty. They helped her to her car and saw her safely on her way. Laney felt a rush of exhaustion strip away her remaining energy. Whatever they had discovered, there would not be any further developments until the morning.

Beckett walked her back to the cabin. Mercifully, he did not say anything further about what had passed between them.

When she was safely inside, she closed the curtains and hoisted Admiral onto her bed, letting him curl into the warmth of her stomach. "You understand why I can't trust Beckett again, right?"

Admiral swiped a tongue under her chin and snuggled closer.

No, Admiral probably couldn't imagine anything of the kind. But what did the dog know of betrayal? He probably didn't even remember the family who had abandoned him at the vet clinic. If the dog could speak, would he chastise her for being foolish? She understood on some level why Beckett asked for the divorce.

But the deep-down, soul-crushing ache of it, being turned away when she'd needed him most, would not subside. *Is it pride, Lord?* On the heels of that prickly thought, she turned out the light and pulled up the quilt.

She awakened with a start. The bedside clock told her it was just before two in the morning. Why had she woken? Though her muscles still ached from her life-or-death run from Kenny's uncle, she was not uncomfortable, nor consumed by a craving or a need to visit the restroom. But there was something, just out of reach in her senses.

The porch light she'd left on at Beckett's insistence created a feeble glow through the front curtains. A shadow crept past the window. Her stomach dropped. It wasn't Beckett gliding past, too short and too stealthy. As quietly as possible, she slid out of bed, leaving Admiral snoring under the blankets. Grabbing her cell phone, she tiptoed to the window, easing the curtain back enough to peer out. The shadow was gone. Had she imagined it? She was tapping out a text message to Beckett when a realization began to dawn on her, something out of place, something dangerous.

Smoke!

She yanked the drapes fully open, sending Admiral into a panic. Gray puffs drifted across the courtyard. Beckett emerged from his tent at a gallop, still fully clothed.

She shoved her feet into some shoes and opened the door, stepping out on the porch and making sure Admiral did not follow. Beckett ran toward her, skidding to a stop as his senses took in the same message. There was a fire...close.

"I'm calling the fire department." Even as she dialed, she realized what Beckett was no doubt recognizing also... The fire was coming from the western set of rooms, from the spot where their one-and-only guest was sleeping.

Beckett sprinted to Rita's room. Smoke poured out from under the door. He didn't bother knocking but tried the handle. Locked. He was hammering on the wood and hollering when Herm arrived, barefoot and sleepy eyed, followed by a fully dressed Levi.

"I was out checking on a horse," Levi said. "Break the window?"

"I'll get a metal chair." Herm turned and hustled off.

Beckett didn't wait. He aimed a massive kick at the spot just below the door handle. It held until the second smash, when the wood splintered and gave, letting loose a plume of acrid smoke.

"Curtains have caught," Levi shouted.

"Rita," Beckett yelled over the fizz and crackle of the burning curtains. "Are you in there?"

Laney pushed through the smoke, a handkerchief held over her mouth. "Don't breathe this stuff in," he called to her, but she shoved a fire extinguisher at him before Herm put down the chair he'd fetched and guided her away.

Spraying the foam as he went, Beckett pushed into the room, Levi right behind him.

At first his eyes stung with the fumes emitted by the burning curtains. "Rita," he shouted.

Levi ran past the neatly made bed into the bathroom. "She's not here."

Gone? But he could just make out her blue vinyl suitcase in the corner. Wherever she was, at least she had not been injured by the smoke. Levi yanked down the curtains and he continued working the extinguisher until the fire was doused, leaving the charred linen remains. There was a blackened mess on the floor, but fortunately nothing else in the room had caught. Beckett directed Laney to cancel the fire department and she made the call.

Beckett and Levi examined the floor. "Wasn't an accident, was it?" Levi asked.

Beckett didn't have to answer. They both knew it wasn't.

"What in the world happened?" Herm said, standing a few paces away with Laney.

"There." Levi pointed at a long, slender wooden stick that stuck out from underneath the ruined curtains. "It's one of those paint-mixing sticks." The end was charred and blackened. "Someone lit it and shoved it under. Caught the curtains."

A high-pitched cry sounded behind

them. They all whirled to see Rita with her hands to her mouth. She carried a backpack over her shoulder. "I couldn't sleep. I was reading in the lodge." The whites of her eyes were wide in the gloom.

"Kenny?" Laney breathed.

Rita didn't answer, staring into the smoke.

Beckett's thoughts raced. Kenny had been on hotel grounds? So very close to where Laney slept and he'd chosen to set fire to Rita's room? The thought both chilled and mystified him.

Rita mouthed something that sounded like, "Pauline was right." He started to ask when a voice interrupted him.

"Fire's out?" Beckett turned to see Trent Clouder in civilian clothes, hustling over with an extinguisher.

"Yes," Beckett said. "Laney canceled the call. Where did you come from?"

He shrugged. "I was on my way home, just finished my shift. I heard over the radio." He laid a hand on Rita's forearm. "Are you all right?"

She answered, her gaze still locked on

the smoke trickling from her room. "I will be, as soon as I get far away from this town."

He squeezed gently. "Are you sure you're okay? You've had a shock. I can drive you to the clinic."

She hitched her backpack higher on her shoulder and stepped away from his touch. "I'm fine. But I can tell you I'm not sleeping in that room. I'll be sitting in the lodge until I can get my car and then I'm gone."

Beckett wanted to press her about the supposed evidence she'd collected from Pauline, but he felt uneasy about bringing it up in front of Clouder. His own feelings puzzled him. Maybe he'd just plain forgotten how to trust people.

"Police are on their way," Herm said.

Rita's mouth tightened. "You all can talk to them. I have nothing to say."

Clouder's tone was soothing, the same Beckett had heard him use on accident victims when they'd been on shift together. "This is upsetting, for sure. Why don't I walk you to the lodge and sit with you for a while?"

"That's not necessary," Rita said.

"It's no problem," he insisted cheerfully. "I'm a night owl and I've got no one waiting for me at home except a goldfish who can't tell time. Beckett can wait for the long arm of the law."

"I'll put the kettle on and make some tea," Herm said. "And fetch you a blanket. It can be chilly in the wee hours."

Rita did not look happy, but she returned to the lodge with Herm and Clouder.

Beckett made sure Laney was far enough away from the stench and settled on a chair before he sent Levi to escort Aunt Kitty back home. "Jude will want to talk. I'll have him call you. No sense standing around here."

Levi nodded. He walked away a few paces before he turned. "Beck?"

Beckett waited. If his taciturn cousin had something to say, it was important.

"Something's not right here." Levi held

his gaze for a long moment before he turned and left.

Not right. And it wasn't merely a vengeful brother.

Pauline was right, Rita had said. About what?

He looked at Laney, who was staring mournfully at the damaged room. He felt the time ticking by, like a burning fuse making its way toward the dynamite.

Figure it out, Beckett. Now.

FOURTEEN

Jude arrived some fifteen minutes later and interviewed Rita before joining them. Both men seemed completely content to stand there in the smoky night until Laney convinced them to return to the cabin, where they sat in the tiny living room. She insisted on fixing decaf coffee, and Jude and Beckett politely sipped the brew. She'd been a disastrous cook when she'd returned to Death Valley after her years in college and working in a Las Vegas hotel. Aunt Kitty taught her the basics, and she could just about manage a pot of coffee, though sometimes she lost count of the scoops. She took one sip and realized she'd done just that, which accounted for the full cups in front of the men. She hoped she'd master more cooking skills by the time the baby arrived. Muffin could not survive on oatmeal-raisin cookies and tamale casserole.

Why had Beckett's nickname for the baby stuck fast? She brought her wandering thoughts back on track. "What did Rita tell you?"

Jude sighed. "I get nothing from her except the cold shoulder. What do you know?"

Beckett and Laney filled him in on their strange conversation with Rita about Pauline's possible ulterior motives in coming to Death Valley.

Jude mulled it over. "I've looked at Pauline's file again. Her landlord said she'd told him when she left for Furnace Falls that her intention was to return in five days. She asked him to collect her mail. We went through it. Nothing of note."

"Cell phone?" Beckett asked.

"None found. Receipts tell us she had one of those pay-as-you-go phones, so we couldn't trace the number anyway." He looked toward the courtyard, the lights of the torches glimmering in the distance.

"Rita knows something," Laney said.

Jude scrubbed a weary hand over his face. "At the moment, I don't have probable cause to get a search warrant for Rita's car or belongings. She hasn't broken any laws, and she isn't a suspect in Pauline's murder."

Beckett flinched, and she knew what he was thinking. *No, just him.*

Her self-control unraveled. After all that had happened, it seemed to her that each moment was of the essence—there must be no more holding back. She put down her coffee. "Jude," she said, "you don't still think Beckett is guilty of Pauline's murder."

His eyes widened in surprise. "That's not what we're talking about here."

"Yes, it is. Rita, Pauline's mysterious mission in Furnace Falls, now this fire… You have to see that there are circumstances behind her death that none of us were aware of."

Jude toyed with the coffee mug.

Beckett lifted a shoulder. "It's okay, Laney."

"No, it's not," she snapped. "You are cousins, family. Maybe you take that for granted because you both had blood relatives who raised you, but I don't. What happened in high school changed you both. It could have brought you closer but instead it ripped you apart. You let it do that. Beckett didn't kill Pauline, Jude, and you know it."

Jude opened his mouth, then closed it. Beckett stared at her until her cheeks went hot and there was something soft and sweet in his gaze.

Jude finally spoke. "I think there is reason to believe Beckett was not at fault."

Laney rolled her eyes, but Beckett broke into a smile.

"That's good enough for me."

Jude quirked a smile. "Good, 'cause that's all you're going to get for now."

Laney sighed. It would have to do. "Now we can move on."

Jude fingered his radio. "I could take another crack at talking to Rita."

Beckett shook his head. "If you do, she'll clam up. We may never find out what she knows."

Laney chewed her lip. "Do you think it was Kenny who started the fire?"

Jude frowned. "Actually, he was spotted at a bar in Beatty two hours ago. That's where I was before I came here. He'd already gone when I arrived. He could have had time to return and set the fire, or get his uncle to do it, but why would he when…?"

"When he's got his original target so close by," Laney finished. "Me."

Beckett glowered as she told him about the shadow moving across her window. She stalled his complaint. "I know I should have mentioned it before, but it just plain slipped my mind. Besides, maybe it's paranoia," she said.

"You should go stay with Aunt Kitty," Beckett said.

Jude chimed in. "Mom would love to have you."

"And who is going to help Herm run this place?" she said.

"I will," Beckett said.

"The last time I left you in charge of the laundry service, the washer exploded and we had suds up and down the hallway."

"I'll read the manual this time."

She shook her head. "I'm staying here. We have a family checking in on Monday." She held up a finger to silence Beckett and Jude. "If I am a target, I'm safer here with Herm and Levi looking out for me."

She was gratified to see Jude nod. "She does have a point. Lots more people around here to keep her in their sights." He got up from the table. "Got work to do. I'll talk to Clouder and see if he can figure anything out from the burn patterns, and I'll assign a unit stationed at the entrance for the rest of the night." He kissed Laney on the cheek. "Stay safe, okay?"

"I will." She shot him a teasing look. "Sure you don't want some coffee to go?"

"Uh, no, thank you."

She laughed and let him out.

Beckett got up from the table. Before she realized what he was up to, he pressed a kiss to her forehead. Her stomach tensed. She'd allowed him to get too close, opened the door for a deeper connection. Anxiety rolled through her in waves.

"Beckett..."

"That's a thank-you kiss."

"To thank me for what?"

"Getting Jude to admit that there might be the slimmest chance that I'm not a murderer after all." She heard the slight hitch in his voice. "I never thought I would hear him say it."

Let it be a new beginning, she prayed. Let God shine a light through the crack she'd just witnessed in his self-loathing. Before she could think it through, she reached up and wrapped her arms around his neck. He went still.

"Do you think...?" he murmured into

her neck. "If I can prove I'm innocent, is there a chance we could...?"

She stopped him with a squeeze, head still pressed under his chin. "I'm not sure," she whispered around a surge of emotion she couldn't name. What did she want? What was God leading her to? Could her tattered heart survive another crushing disappointment?

He gulped in a breath, pressed another kiss to her temple that lingered, and straightened. "I won't push. It's enough for me that you didn't say flat-out no. I know I hurt you and broke your trust, but if there's the slightest possibility that I can have a second chance, I will be content with that."

"I didn't know you wanted another chance," she managed. "You were going to leave."

"I didn't think I deserved one, but now..."

"Now?"

"I'm not sure, but I'm feeling just reckless enough to ask."

"Because there's a baby?"

His eyes roved her face. "You said that I never talk about how I feel, so I'll say it. The baby is a part of it, yes."

Of course. The baby. He didn't want to walk away from his duty as a father. She started to turn away when the flood of tears started. "I don't want to talk any more about this now."

"Laney…"

"I'm tired."

"Okay." He sighed. "Good night."

He left and she stood there, immobile, Admiral licking her ankle.

Why hadn't she flat out said there was no future for them? Confusion? She'd not wanted to hurt him?

Or was she too considering a second chance? Maybe he was allowing God to change him in some fundamental way. But God would have to change her in a profound way as well, to overcome the chasm of mistrust in her soul. She would not restart a life with Beckett just because he wanted to be close to the baby.

The conversation twisted round and round in her mind, leaving her unable to sleep. Her stomach called. Ice cream. Nature's perfect food. She crept out of bed and headed for the mini fridge and freezer where she kept her supply of chocolate ripple. Realizing she had left the shades open, she went to close them, startled to see Beckett laid out on the hard wooden bench, one arm flung over his head in sleep. His tall frame was too long for the furniture, and he had to prop his booted feet on the bench arm.

He'd decided the tent was too far away to protect her properly. How comfortable could it be after the battering he'd taken at the borax mines? Gathering up a soft quilt and a pillow, she tiptoed onto the porch and unfolded it gently over him.

He stirred, eyes flying wide, mouth open to speak.

"Don't talk," she ordered. "Just follow directions."

He raised an eyebrow. "But…"

"Quiet."

He closed his mouth.

"If you're going to be stubborn and sleep on the bench, at least lift up your head," she directed.

He did so and she slid the pillow into position. He didn't reach out to touch her, or talk, but his smile was stunning in the darkness, a silent thank-you that made him look like a love-struck teen.

Love struck.

He loves you? Or he wants you back because of the baby?

There would be plenty of time to think about that in the morning.

She'd had enough angst for one day.

Beckett folded the blanket and stacked the pillow neatly on top. Levi had kept an eye on the cabin while he'd showered, shaved, fixed a pot of coffee and checked on Rita, who was asleep on a sofa in the lodge.

In a dreamlike state, he remembered Laney draping him with a blanket and her response when he'd asked for a second chance.

Was it possible she might consider it? She was not the same woman he'd proposed to and married. She was stronger somehow; her first priority was the wee life tucked in the merest bump of her belly. He found this different Laney to be even more breathtaking than the one he'd known. And he was changed too, wasn't he? Wasn't God showing him that he could be a different man through Laney? He had let what happened in high school mold his perception of himself.

But Laney said there was no condemnation...not from God and not from her...for what he'd done to Dan. *No condemnation.*

Two words that gave him a sliver of hope.

Laney opened the door of the cabin, emerging in leggings and one of his oversize T-shirts that had to be the most fetching outfit he'd ever clapped eyes on.

"Are you staring?" she asked.

"No," he said, handing her a cup of decaf. "I like the outfit, that's all."

She groaned. "I might have gained too much this week, on account of the shake and a few other snacks I won't admit to. Dr. Irene will scold me."

"She won't dare."

"She might. We're good enough friends that we can tell each other things."

He pulled at his baseball cap. "You've talked about me plenty, huh?"

She went pink and he hastened to reply.

"It's okay. I'm glad you had someone. It must have been brutal when I was arrested."

"It was brutal when you stopped taking my calls or letting me see you."

He swallowed the shame. "I'm sorry."

She sipped the coffee as they walked back to the lodge. A frown creased her forehead. Regret from what she'd said the night before? He couldn't bear it, but he couldn't stand not knowing either.

"Are you okay?"

She let out a sigh. "I always feel anxious

on doctor appointment days, even when there isn't a killer lurking and fires burning or..."

Or reliving her husband's betrayal. He took her hand. "Muffin is strong, like her mama."

She smiled. "You think it's a girl too?"

"Man's intuition."

She fired a look of mock surprise at him. "Men have intuition? I didn't know that."

"We like to tell ourselves we do, anyway."

In the lodge, Herm was sitting at the table, eating a plate of scrambled eggs and reading a fishing magazine. "Fix you something?" he asked, half rising.

"No," she reassured him. "I have to fast for a blood test." She peeked into the sitting room. Rita's suitcase had been rescued from the smoke and delivered to the lodge, where it sat next to the door. "Where's Rita?"

"Just stepped into the bathroom, I think.

Clouder stayed with her until she fell asleep."

"That was nice of him," Laney said.

Beckett finished his coffee when Rita came into the kitchen looking rumpled and sleepy.

"I'm going to call a taxi to take me to town," she said. "What's the local company?"

"No need. I'm driving Laney to a doctor's appointment at noon, but I can drive you before then or Herm might be up for it."

"Course," Herm said. "Happy to."

She looked uneasy. "No, really, it's fine. I'll find my own way."

"It's the least we can do after what happened," Laney said.

"No," Rita snapped. She must have realized the abruptness of her tone. "Thank you, but I will find my own way."

She looked uneasy as a chicken in a fox hole. Worried about Kenny? It still made no sense what had happened the night before. She had the answers and it was killing him not to interrogate her, and he could not hold back the question. "What about the proof, about Pauline?"

She shook her head. "Like I said, as soon as I'm safely away from here, I'll call you."

"How do we know you'll do it?"

"You don't. Truth is I'm not interested in bringing a killer to justice or anything so noble. The matter will be yours to deal with. You can follow through and we'll all be safer with a murderer off the streets."

Beckett's stomach tensed. She knew the answer, the key that would free him and ensure Laney's safety. He stepped forward to press her but caught Laney's frown. She was right. If he spooked her, they might never know.

Instead he handed her a business card with the name of a taxi company. "If you're sure I can't take you."

She took the card and disappeared back into the lodge. He resisted the urge to run after her. *Let her go*, he thought, *but keep her in your sights for as long as you can.*

He telephoned Jude to fill him in on Rita's plans.

When the cab pulled onto the property, she stood by with her purse, ready to go. He opened the passenger door and helped her in.

She gave him a long look. "I'm sorry. I never should have gotten involved in this."

Then the taxi driver started the engine and drove off.

Had he allowed his only chance at redemption to hop into a taxi and ride away?

No, he hadn't been given hope just to have it all stripped away again.

Muscles taut, he returned to the hotel.

FIFTEEN

Laney peered into the front window of the mechanic's shop as Beckett drove them along the quiet street. She pulled the ratty sweater closer around herself, though it was not at all cold. It was like some sort of armor, that tattered sweater with the lighter in the pocket and the sewn-up hole in the elbow. A vein jumped in Beckett's jaw as he idled the truck at the corner.

"I don't see her. She must have gotten her car and left town." He drummed on the steering wheel. "Maybe I should have tried to follow her."

"That wouldn't have helped. We've got to wait it out and see if she makes good on her word." Waiting, ugh.

He huffed out a breath. "I'm not content relying on her word."

"Me neither, but Jude is checking her out closely now too."

They pulled into the parking lot of the doctor's office.

The nurse greeted them. "Hello, Mrs. Duke. Please come on back to the exam room."

Beckett hesitated. "Can I...? I mean, am I allowed?"

Laney felt her face flood with color before she nodded.

"Wait right here," the nurse said. "I'll get her settled, get a blood sample and call you in, okay?"

When Irene entered twenty minutes later, she ushered Beckett in too. Irene was her usual upbeat self, but there was concern written in the lines around her mouth. "Sorry I'm late." She looked harried. "Before we get around to baby business, what happened last night? I heard from Trent this morning that you had a fire."

"Trent Clouder?" Laney said with an eyebrow raised. "You just happened to run into him?"

Irene pulled a face. "Okay, we had breakfast together at the café." She put on a pair of glasses. "Before you start, it was a friendly chat, nothing more."

"Sounds like a date to me," Laney said.

"You're evading the question." She assisted Laney onto the table with a pillow behind her neck.

"Somebody set fire to Rita's room," Beckett said.

Her eyes widened. "Is it Kenny?"

"We don't know," Beckett said.

She paused with her stethoscope in hand. "Wait a minute. You told me that this Rita woman was trying to dig up dirt about Pauline's murder. Did she uncover something?"

"She might have a way to prove Beckett innocent," Laney said.

Irene gaped. "Really? How?"

Beckett shot her a warning look.

"I can't say any more, but I'm just hanging on to the hope that this nightmare might be over at long last," she said.

"Absolutely. We need this baby to come into a bright new world for his or her parents." Irene winked at Laney. "Both of them."

Touché. It was Laney's turn to squirm.

Irene listened to Laney's heart with her stethoscope and took blood while Beckett hovered. She typed notes in her computer file. "Speaking of baby business, let's see how our customer is doing today, shall we?"

Irene called her nurse, who held the ultrasound wand. "Your next appointment is all checked in, Doctor."

"I thought Laney was my last one."

The nurse shook her head. "Nope. You have two more back-to-back since we had to cancel two earlier."

Laney grinned. "Dates take precedence."

Irene groaned. "I can remember when I was thrilled to have two or three appointments a day."

She directed the nurse, who began to move the wand around. "There's the bambino," Irene said. "Pretty as a picture." She clicked the computer and took some measurements, which she also recorded in her chart. Laney watched the tiny figure on the screen. At first, she could not decipher what she was seeing.

"Here are the head and the feet," Irene said. "One arm up. Baby is waving."

Laney watched the wiggling figure. Out of the corner of her eye, she saw Beckett go pale as he looked at their child. His bug-eyed stare went from the screen to Dr. Irene and back again.

"Is…everything okay? All that stuff you're writing down?" he said.

"Yes. I'm a compulsive note taker. I learned that early on. Your baby is a perfect four-month specimen. Would you like to know the gender?"

"No," Beckett and Laney said at exactly the same moment.

"Okay, then." Irene sat back and glanced

at her nurse. "Would you tell my next appointment I'll be there in a moment?"

The nurse excused herself.

"I've got a full schedule, otherwise I would join you for a break. I'm afraid to let you out of my sight with all that's gone on."

Laney's heart swelled at her dear friend. "No problem. We have to go, but I'll have the coffee ready next time you're out running."

Irene glanced over her shoulder at Beckett and smiled. "It may take some time for him to snap out of it."

He was ogling the strip of paper photos printed from the ultrasound machine that she'd left next to her computer. He was quite oblivious to anything else. Irene squeezed Laney's hand. "Talk to you later."

Laney sat up on the exam table and pulled the gown around her. "Beckett?" Astonished, she realized that two perfect tears were sliding down his tanned cheeks.

He tore his gaze from the paper and looked at her. "That's our baby," he croaked.

"Yes," she said.

"And in five months, you're going to deliver him or her."

"Yes, that is how it works in all the books I've read."

He didn't crack a smile. Slowly, millimeter by millimeter, his gaze moved from the screen to her face. She realized with a fright that he had actually begun to sway on his feet. Grabbing the hospital gown around herself with one hand, she leaped from the table and shoved him into a chair with the other.

He collapsed into it and she pushed his head down between his knees. "Breathe deep. Come on. Three breaths in and out."

He complied. She was considering calling the nurse back in when he sat up again, looking dazed, but fully conscious.

"Laney," he said.

"What?"

"This is real, isn't it?"

Laney blinked back a wash of tears. "As real as it gets, Beckett."

Beckett insisted on stopping at the store to buy some ingredients to make a special dinner.

"Herm has the night off from cooking," he said. He was going to suggest he cook her favorite trout dish with the capers and almonds, but the last time he'd fixed it for her had been the weekend before the murder. It was time to start making some new memories, or at least, treating her to something nice while they waited to see if Rita would make good on her promise. "What would you like?"

When she finished declining for the second time, she blew out a breath and said, "Pancakes."

He blinked. "Pancakes? Not steak or fancy pasta?"

"Pancakes," she repeated. "With gallons of maple syrup. And butter. Real butter, not margarine."

He could not restrain his delight. She

wanted pancakes. This woman, amazing and strong, had an actual child growing inside her. God had gifted them with the impossible. The sheer incredulity of it made his head spin again. "All right." Since they had all the fixings for pancakes at the hotel, he drove straight there. She was yawning by the time they returned.

"I need a nap, I think," Laney said.

"Great idea. I want to check on some things anyway."

"If it were me, you'd tell me to stay out of trouble."

He laughed. "And if it were you, you wouldn't listen to me at all."

Now she laughed and the sun caught the dimple in her cheek and gilded her hair to molten platinum. "See you later."

She was almost over the threshold when she stopped and turned. "Here," she said.

He took the strip of ultrasound pictures. "You want me to have them?"

"Yes. There will be more, but you should have these."

He stared as she closed the door. What

did the offering mean? That he wasn't going to be included in the rest of the pregnancy? Had she already decided she would not allow him back into her life? Or was it a tender gesture, since he'd made such a grand fool out of himself when he'd clapped eyes on the baby's image in the first place?

He wasn't sure, but he went to his tent and tucked the paper carefully in his Bible. No matter what happened, he would have the pictures close, a present from the woman who had been his greatest gift.

With a lighter step than he'd felt in forever, he began to tinker around the courtyard. He yearned to start on the repairs to the burned room, but he did not want to be out of sight of Laney's door. He contented himself leveling some stepping-stones that had become askew. He thought about the screw Aunt Kitty had discovered. Had Rita found something Pauline left behind, a second copy of whatever incriminating info she'd been using to blackmail someone?

Who? It had to have been a local, someone who knew their way around Death Valley, someone who had known Pauline would reach out to Beckett? Or perhaps the note to arrange the meeting with Pauline that fateful night had been written by the killer in the first place.

Before he realized it, the afternoon had passed and he'd reset the entire walkway, correcting all the crooked stones and adding new gravel to the low spots. He couldn't have Laney or the child tripping.

Laney, his Laney. The thought was audacious, breathtaking. Could he possibly believe he might put his family back together with God's help? Was he worthy of such a treasure? Laney emerged with Admiral at her heels as the sun mellowed toward evening.

She eyed his work. "You've been productive. Are you rebuilding from the ground up?"

Maybe, just maybe, he was. He shrugged. "Keeping busy, but I'm ready for pancakes. How about you?"

They entered the kitchen. He found the

flour container empty. "Be right back." The finicky basement door was slightly ajar. He jogged down steps. The fourth one was still wobbly. A few of the newspapers piled there were knocked over, so he straightened them before fetching the flour.

In the kitchen he whistled as he whisked up the ingredients. A sizzle of butter, perfect scoops of batter into the pan and, in a few moments, he'd cooked up a platter of golden pancakes. She'd retrieved the required jug of syrup.

She reached for his hand to say grace. She thanked the Lord for the food, while he expressed silent gratitude for her presence.

Laney had always been a fairly light eater, but she polished off her first pancake and he forked her a second one.

"Don't tell Doc Irene?"

"My lips are sealed."

The sweetness dancing along his senses had nothing to do with the maple syrup. They talked, chatted with relative ease.

The kitchen was the same old worn space, but he felt like a different person, looking at a woman who was both the same woman he'd married and completely new to him, so strong, so incredibly brave.

When the meal came to an end, he didn't want their time together to cease. They washed up the dishes, side by side, and tidied until there was nothing left to do.

"Thank you for the pancakes," she said. "Muffin approves."

He dared to reach out and stroke her hair, soft as downy feathers. "I forgot."

Her breath had gone shallow. "Forgot what?"

"How soft your hair is."

She leaned in and then stopped. "Maybe this isn't a good idea."

He closed the gap between them and kissed her. He felt her warm to the kiss, her lips the same perfect fit he remembered.

She broke off and looked at him searchingly. "You seem different, Beckett."

"How so?"

"I don't know exactly. It's like you believe all of a sudden."

"Believe what? That I'll be cleared of this mess? We're a long way from that."

"No, it's like you found a part of yourself that you lost a long time ago, back in high school."

He didn't want to move. Instead he wanted to stay there, drinking in her eyes and the small hope that burned deep down in them. "I... I'm trying."

She cupped his cheek. "Keep trying," she whispered. "No matter what happens. Remember that you are who God says you are." And then she kissed him again, a quick kiss, but so much the more meaningful because she'd initiated it. She turned to go and stopped quickly, bent slightly.

He was next to her in a flash. "What? What is it? What's wrong?"

When she straightened, tears glazed her cheeks. "I... I felt the baby move." Her tears continued to stream unchecked as he embraced her, and he added a few of his own. Heart thumping in a joyful cascade, he saw her safely to the cabin.

You are who God says you are.

It was time to make things right.

He picked up the phone and made a call to arrange a long-overdue meeting.

SIXTEEN

She awoke a few hours later. A residual glow from the pancake dinner still kindled in her veins. And to think that the first time she'd felt their baby move, Beckett had been there with her. What did it all mean? Was God telling her to open her heart again? Could she even if she decided to? Like Beckett, she had her own invisible wound, a scar left when her foster family had made it clear they were not the forever family she'd craved.

They'd stopped wanting her, and she'd told herself that Beckett had too. But the man she'd shared pancakes with, who'd nearly sacrificed his life for hers at the borax works, was not that same man.

Had he changed, or had she? Though she prayed for clarity, none came.

She went to the window, expecting to see Beckett snoozing under the quilt. Instead she found Officer Norris sitting with his gaze fixed out into the night. She opened the door.

"Hello, Officer. I didn't expect to see you here. Where's Beckett?"

"He called and asked for someone to hang out here until he got back."

"Got back from where?"

"I don't know, ma'am, but he called to tell me he's on his way. He'll be here in about a half hour."

"All right. Thank you." Puzzled, she closed the door. What errand would have been so important to take him away from the hotel, especially while they were eagerly awaiting word from Rita?

She kept watch for his arrival. Just before nine, he pulled up and parked, shook Norris's hand, and the officer drove away. She pulled on a sweater and her roomiest sweatpants and opened the door. Admiral cracked a sleepy eye, slogged off the bed and followed.

He greeted her, startled. "I thought you'd be asleep."

"Me too. Where did you go?"

"I..."

Admiral let out a bark and trotted off as fast as his stubby legs would carry him.

"No, Admiral, stop," Laney cried. The dog disappeared between the lodge and the west wing of rooms. Beckett and Laney followed, but Admiral was spry for an elderly canine, and he made off into the woods behind the property.

Laney clapped a hand to her forehead. "Oh, he's simply fixated on this tree full of squirrels that live on the far side of the woods."

"That same tree he was fascinated with back in the winter?"

She quirked a smile, pleased that he remembered such a small detail. "Yes. He'll keep going until he's half dead of exhaustion, unless I stop him."

"I'll take the truck and drive around

to the road. You shouldn't be out here at night."

"I'd better go with you. No offense, but he's not going to come when you call."

Beckett laughed. "Now, that I believe. We'll go together, but you're not getting out of the truck. I'll call Levi too and have him help out if we need to widen the search party."

The night was shifting from slate gray to black, the stars beginning to poke through the velvety sky. She wanted to ask him about his mysterious errand, but she had to keep her eyes peeled for any sign of her AWOL companion.

They reached the small bridge that separated the hotel property from the vast wild expanse behind theirs. At the far side of the stone structure was the sprawling ancient oak, home to Admiral's rodent nemeses. She rolled down the window and yelled.

Hearing no reply, she hollered again. Admiral zinged out from the shrubbery, whining pitifully. Her skin prickled. "Admiral, come here, baby."

But the dog turned back into the shrubs.

"Naughty thing," she breathed.

Levi rode up on his mare, a flashlight in his hand. Willow followed him on a smaller horse. "We were watching a movie," she said. "Figured a double set of eyes would be better. Levi can't always find the milk in the fridge, so I figured…"

Levi smirked at her. "Thanks, sis."

"You're welcome. Found him yet? I heard whining when we got close, or maybe that was Levi."

Laney would have laughed at the sibling gibes, but worry was worming its way through her nerves. She leaned out the window. "Come here right now, Admiral," she hollered in her best "I mean business" voice.

The dog did not come.

"What is he so interested in out there?" she whispered. Would the squirrels be active at night? Dread began to tingle deep in her belly.

"Stay here," Beckett said to Laney. "Levi, will you stay too?"

Levi nodded. Laney noted the rifle secured to his saddle and swallowed hard.

"I'm going with you, Beckett," Willow said, "so let's not waste any more time." She pulled a revolver from her saddlebag and tucked it into her pocket.

Willow had been the victim of violence, so she never traveled too far without protection. But guns? Surely this was just a naughty misbehaving dog, wasn't it? The thought rang false.

Willow followed Beckett on horseback until the branches made the way impassable. She dismounted and looped the reins over a tree branch.

Laney felt the night suddenly grow cold as the two vanished into the darkness.

Beckett homed in on the sound of Admiral's whining. It grew louder as they approached a small clearing.

"Beck," Willow said. She flashed her light on the ground, illuminating a smashed swatch of grass. "It looks like something was dragged here." Her voice was a whisper, but it sounded in his gut like a warning Klaxon. A moment like this had changed his life.

He swallowed down the memory of finding Pauline not very far from their current location, her lifeless hands flung up as if to ward off her death.

Admiral's whine was shrill and sharp, close.

"Come here, boy."

This time, the dog did as requested, hobbling out of the shadows over to Beckett, pawing at his knee. When he bent to hoist him up, Admiral turned and darted to a low-lying set of pine branches.

"Beck..." Willow screamed.

From under the branches protruded a set of legs, a woman's jean-covered legs, twisted at an unnatural angle. A tiny glimpse of braid shone in the flashlight gleam, Rita's braid. They ran, Beckett yanking up the branches. Willow bent to press her fingers to the exposed wrist.

Minutes turned into lifetimes as he waited.

"She's dead," Willow said. At the same time, their gazes traveled to an object close to Rita's outstretched hand.

A cap, a Furnace Falls Fire Department baseball cap, stained and battered.

His cap.

A second scream severed the night like a blade. He jerked around to see Laney standing with her hand to her mouth, Levi right behind her. She looked from the dead woman to Beckett. Slowly her gaze came to rest on the baseball cap.

"Please tell me this isn't happening again." Her eyes were huge, pleading, desperate.

He could only stare at her, wishing with all his power that he had any other answer to give her.

She was sitting in the truck with Admiral on her lap when Jude and Officer Norris arrived. Though she wore her trusty sweater, she was shivering. Jude lifted a hand to her, his face grim as granite. More officers arrived, a team from the coroner's office. The nightmare continued. After Jude talked to Willow and Levi, Levi rode his mare away, leading Willow's. Willow climbed into the driver's side of the truck and reached over to squeeze Laney's shoulder.

"You know he didn't do this. They won't be able to find any proof."

Except Beckett's hat at the murder scene?

Jude approached after a while and she listened to him through the open window.

"Laney, was Beckett on the property all night?"

"I…" She shook her head. "He went out for a while. I don't know where. But he did not kill Rita. Why would he? She was going to give us information to clear him from Pauline's death, once and for all." She broke off and tried to catch her breath.

He laid his hand on hers where she gripped the door frame. "We'll get it straightened out. I'm going to take Beckett to the station to get a statement and we'll see where it goes from there."

"I'm coming."

"Laney..." Beckett was still six feet away, no doubt at Jude's request. "Go home. I don't want you involved in this."

Go back home and walk away from whatever had been building between them?

Press in and embroil herself and her baby in another horror?

Did she have the strength to face it? To draw close and have him push her away again? Did she even love him still or was it the stubborn ties of the past? She drew in a breath and made her decision, pushing the door open so suddenly Jude had to sidestep.

"Laney..." Jude started, but she ignored him.

Beckett's face was grooved with the deepest despair and disbelief. Pain radiated off him in palpable waves. She marched to him and tipped her chin up, locking eyes with his.

"I am still your wife, technically. I will not walk away from you." She caught the sparkle of moisture in his eyes and she knew hers were damp too.

He opened his mouth to speak, his hands reaching for her, but Jude had caught up and gently moved her back. "If you want to come to the station, I won't stop you, but it will be a long night."

She got back into the truck.

Willow was already in the driver's seat. "I'll take you. We can drop Admiral off on the way."

Willow didn't try to make conversation as they drove to the station. What was there to say? They'd heard more commotion before they'd left the woods, and she knew they'd found Rita's car in a tangle of shrubbery. The police would do a thorough examination, check it for fingerprints and fibers and such. She tried to think calmly, as they settled into the uncomfortable chairs in the police station lobby. Beckett's hat at the scene wasn't enough to lead to his arrest, was it?

She was filled with frenetic energy and wanted to pace, but the space was small and Willow was already prowling around the dingy spot, making calls to Levi, Aunt Kitty, Herm.

Laney should be thinking about those details also, but it was as if her brain was stuck in a hopeless groove. *Lord, how could it be? Again.* It was happening all over; nothing had changed.

But her whole world had changed. There was a baby inside her, a tiny God-given life. And she'd thought something had begun to shift in Beckett too.

"Poor Rita," she whispered. A young woman killed, discarded like a piece of trash, her death used to frame an innocent man. Had Kenny done it to punish Beckett? Kenny was a brutal man, but he didn't seem the type to work out a plan to frame Beckett. His modus operandi had been more direct so far.

The longer the door to the interrogation room stayed closed, the worse she felt. Fatigue and despair began to overwhelm her like sand piling up in the dunes.

When the door opened, she bolted to her feet. Jude ushered Beckett down the hall and buzzed him into the waiting room. He had the dazed look of a sleepwalker.

"You're free to go, Beckett," Jude said.

"You're...you're releasing him?" she squeaked.

Jude nodded, the barest hint of relief on his face. "He has an alibi."

Laney noticed in astonishment that another man was behind Jude. Neatly trimmed hair, nicely dressed in khakis and a polo shirt, holding a red-tipped white cane. She knew at once who it had to be: Dan Wheatly, the man Beckett had blinded in the high school wrestling match.

The impact of it left her speechless.

"Hello," he said. "I'm Dan. Beckett was visiting me last night. You must be Laney." He grinned, holding out his hand. "I'm legally blind, but I can see shadows, enough to fool people."

Stunned, she reached out to greet him. "Beckett was visiting you?"

He nodded. "As a matter of fact, Rita called Beckett's cell phone while he was with me. Interrupted our conversation, if only for a brief moment before the call was dropped. The call record of the phone found on her body proves it. It wasn't possible for Beckett to have made it back to Furnace Falls to kill her in that amount of time."

Willow grinned. "So you're Beckett's alibi?"

Dan gave a thumbs-up. "More than that, I'm his new lawyer. It's time for my client to be going home now. Thank you for your time, Sheriff Duke."

Laney followed Beckett to the parking lot. Her senses were clouded, but Beckett gripped her arm and kept her moving.

Behind them, Willow was in deep conversation with Dan. A driver sat behind the wheel of Dan's car. "Would you like a ride home?" Dan asked Willow. "I think maybe Laney and Beckett need to talk and we can catch up on our old high school memories."

She agreed, hugging Laney and Beckett before climbing into the car.

Dan patted Laney on the shoulder. "Things are likely to get worse before they get better. You've got a killer working very hard to destroy your family. And word's already gotten out via the police scanner, so..."

"So the townsfolk who hated me before are boiling the tar and bagging the feathers," Beckett said.

"Something like that," he said. "Don't let your guard down."

Beckett drove out of the police station parking lot. Was it her imagination, or did the few cars on the road at that hour seem to slow and peer closely at them?

She pulled her sweater around her more tightly and kept her gaze out the window, willing the drive to go quickly.

SEVENTEEN

Beckett didn't trust himself to talk, so he kept his jaws clamped together.

Laney was silent for a full three blocks. When she finally did speak, her question wasn't what he'd thought it might be.

"You went to see Dan. Why?"

"No point in talking about that now." The despair came through, though he tried to squash it.

"I want to know."

"Laney…" He broke off, without the energy to resist. "I had to tell him I was sorry."

"Now? After all this time?"

"You said… I mean, you told me that I'd let myself be defined by what people said about me when…when I blinded him in high school. I wanted to tell him that I wasn't that monster back then, I didn't ever mean to hurt him and I have hated myself for it every day of my life."

"What did he say?"

The wonder of it still pulsed through him, floating for a moment, just above the despair. "He said he'd known that all along. He has a great life and he doesn't harbor any resentment." He gulped. "He said he'd been praying for me all these years." Praying...for him. Beckett could hardly still believe it.

"Oh, Beckett." She caught his hand in hers.

He squeezed her fingers and swallowed hard. "Hardly seems to matter now, though."

"It matters," she whispered. "It matters."

They lapsed into silence again until they hit the twists and turns just before Furnace Falls.

"Rita called you when you were with Dan?" she finally asked.

He'd been so lost in his mental morass,

her words startled him. "Yes. It was only a couple of seconds, no more. She said something that sounded like *It's still there* and then the call cut off."

Laney cocked her head. "What could that mean?"

He hesitated. Was it fair to even mention it? Could he possibly stomach creating false hope? He couldn't believe she was even sitting next to him. Her expression in the woods, the agony written there, killed him afresh.

Please tell me this isn't happening again.

But there had been the other moment seared into his soul when she'd walked straight to him. *I am still your wife, technically. I will not walk away from you.* He realized then how badly he'd erred in asking for the divorce. It was the ultimate betrayal, an abandonment of the vows he'd made before her and God, born of his underestimation of her. But if he'd learned anything in the past week, it was that Laney Duke was much stronger than he could ever imagine.

He pulled in a breath. "I thought it might mean that Rita had left whatever proof she might have had behind."

Laney's eyes opened wide. "You think it could be at the hotel?"

"I'm not sure. Jude said there was nothing in Rita's car. I heard them talking at the crime scene. They think she might have been locked in her own trunk. She may have managed to make the call from there before she was killed, probably by a blow to the head with her own tire iron."

"It's so terrible. She must have been so scared. Who could have done it? It had to be the person implicated by whatever Rita had." She chewed her lip. "But maybe this proof is still at the hotel—maybe it never left. There was nothing in her room, unless we missed it."

"I'm going to go through it again, but, Laney, there's so little chance I'm going to find anything to help."

"Little chance is better than zero chance," she said firmly.

He pulled in a breath from deep down.

"You standing by me…" He swallowed and tried again. "I was wrong to push you away before."

Her chin went up, showcasing the slight tremble in her lower lip. "Yes, you were."

He smiled. "Thank you for being here now."

"You're welcome."

He would not bring up what was in his heart, the yearning that had caused him to reach out to Dan after decades. There could be no future between them with Rita's murder and Kenny's threats. The injustice of it burned a path inside him. His only hope was to locate whatever Rita had left, if there really was anything to find.

A flash of headlights caught his attention in the rearview mirror.

Traffic on this road was minimal. Was it Willow come to check on them? Not at this late hour after she'd just left. Levi would have waited at the hotel for them.

Laney, alerted to his tension, looked in the side mirror. "They're getting closer."

He pressed the gas, taking the next turn much faster than he normally would.

Who was closing in behind them? Kenny? A nameless killer? Townspeople who'd heard about the second woman he'd been accused of murdering?

He accelerated. The silvered foothills whizzed past at dizzying speeds. "Call..."

But she was already dialing Jude.

"Dispatching help now," Jude snapped over the speakerphone. "Got a guy close. Stay on the line with me."

He could get no more than a dim outline of the car, no sense of the driver, but he had a feeling he knew who it was.

"Beckett," Laney breathed.

A figure was pushing through the sunroof in the car behind them. There was a flicker of light, as a fuse caught flame, illuminating Kenny, his face ghoulish.

"Close your window," he hollered, bracing as Kenny lobbed the Molotov cocktail in an overhand toss. It shattered in the back of Beckett's truck; flames whooshed up for a moment and then died away.

"He's still behind us," Laney screamed.

He punched the gas harder. Around the next corner they heard the sound of sirens. Kenny must have heard it too because he immediately fell off the pursuit, dropping away into the darkness until he disappeared. Beckett slowed to a safer speed, allowing the police car ahead of them to roll up alongside.

Beckett reported what had happened.

The officer nodded. "Couple of places he might have pulled out. I'll check."

Lights still strobing, he drove away. Beckett made sure the fire was completely gone before he got back in the truck.

His heart was pounding, hands clenched tight on the wheel. "Laney," he gasped. "Please."

She must have known what he was asking. "You want me to leave." It was the barest of whispers and it cut him to the marrow.

"Honey, it's too dangerous at the hotel, too isolated. I can't risk you and the baby getting hurt. I can't let that happen. I won't."

Her lip quivered and she looked at her lap. "I don't want to leave you."

"Hearing you say that means everything to me." His voice broke as he said it. "I will find a way out of this." *I will find a way back to you.*

She cried softly as he captured her hand again. "I'll take you to the hotel to put a bag together and pick up Admiral, okay? Herm can cancel any reservations. I'll drive you to stay with Aunt Kitty. Levi and Willow can take turns hanging out there until things settle down. Just for a while."

How long was a while? Days? Months? Forever?

If that was what it took, he would have to learn to live with it, but he knew right then that he would never give up.

Laney tried not to cry as she packed a small bag. Beckett was talking to Herm in the courtyard. It was only just after midnight, but she was bone tired. It took all her will not to sink down onto the bed and wail. She was leaving her home and Beckett, and it felt like her heart was being ripped out in quivering chunks.

It was not faithfulness, or sentiment, that kept her tied to him. A supply of new tenderness had welled up to fill the scars and wounds he'd left behind. Maybe it wasn't love exactly—she wasn't actually sure what it would feel like to love again—but whatever it was, she was loath to leave. Why would the Lord fill her with such healing, grant them a child and then tear them apart again?

"He wouldn't," she muttered to herself. "He will find us in the middle of this mess." She believed it; she trusted Him, and at the moment, it was the only thing she could cling to. A rap on the door made her wipe her eyes.

"Laney?" Irene stuck her head in, doctor bag in her hand. "I saw all the activity at the police station from my window.

I called Trent and made him tell me. I'm so sorry."

The floodgates opened and all the tears she had been trying to restrain emerged in a mighty rush. Beckett came in, looking uneasily between the two women. "Things are all settled with Herm. We can go anytime. But, um, it can wait a few minutes."

Irene continued to pat Laney. "Beckett, I'm sorry. Truly sorry."

"Thanks for coming."

She nodded. "I figured maybe I'd do a house call in case I could be of help."

Beckett's phone rang and he answered. "No, it's okay. Just leave it there. Thanks, Herm." He stuck his phone in his pocket. "Wait." He jerked his chin to one side as if he'd been struck.

"What is it?" Irene said. "Do you need to sit down?"

Was he ill? "Beckett?" Laney called, moving to him.

He stared at her. "I think I figured out where Rita might have hidden the proof."

Laney felt as if she must have been

dreaming. She gave herself a shake. "How could you know that?"

"Herm just called to ask me if he should store the patio cushions in the basement since there's a storm forecast. It got me to thinking about our pancake dinner. When I went to fetch the flour from the basement, the door was slightly open."

"It doesn't shut properly," Laney explained to Irene. "We've all learned how to lift the handle while we're closing it."

"Right, but it hadn't been closed like that. It had to have been shut by someone who didn't know the door trick."

She could not stop the hope that fluttered in her body like a clumsy baby bird on its first flight. Could it be? Or were they grasping at straws?

"And you think Rita left some kind of proof down there?" Irene said. "About Pauline's murder?"

"Going to find out." Beckett pulled his phone out and called Levi to ask him to come over. He disconnected. "He'll be here in ten minutes."

Irene whistled. "This is just like a treasure hunt."

"Go," Laney urged. "Look right now before something else happens. I'll be fine here. I'll lock the door and Levi will be here in a flash."

"I..."

She took him by the shirtfront and gave him a shake. "Please."

"I'll stay with her until Levi comes," Irene put in. "After all this drama, I can't leave now, can I? You two are much more exciting than the paperwork I have waiting back home."

"Lock the door behind me." Beckett waited until they did so. Through the window, she matched his half-raised hand. So many emotions were in that tired face... hope, anxiety, fear...and something else that lent a softness to it.

Irene joined her at the window to watch Beckett sprint into the darkness.

"It's all going to end soon," Irene said softly.

Could Laney dare believe it? She felt a sudden prick on her neck.

And darkness closed around her too.

EIGHTEEN

Beckett smacked on the light and took the basement stairs two at a time. He started examining the shelf of jams Aunt Kitty had spent last summer putting up. The first shelf revealed nothing. He started in on the lower section, peering behind string beans and tomatoes, checking underneath dozens of batches of pickles. Again, nothing out of place.

Had he been wrong? Rita's message was meant to relay something else? He shoved down the prickle of worry as he started in on the next section, extra flour, a sack of sugar, a massive jug of maple syrup. Where might Rita have hidden something? Everything was neatly in place, concealing nothing.

Was it possible he'd misheard her altogether? Had his ears constructed a scenario to give his heart a shred of hope? He
continued to prowl and poke. The stack
of newspaper sat on the floor, the top a
recent issue that no one had time to read.
He could imagine the next day's headline.

Second Murdered Woman Found on
Hotsprings Hotel Property. And the stain
of it, the suspicion that would stick to
Beckett would cling to Laney, as well.

"It's gotta be here," he muttered.

He ruffled quickly through the newspapers. Underneath the bottom issue, his
fingers found a packet a couple of inches
thick. Breath held, he slid it free. It was
a large manila envelope marked *Beckett* on the front. With hands gone cold,
he undid the clasp. There was a neatly
wrapped stash of a dozen or so clear bags,
filled with labeled pills…gabapentin, pro-
methazine, bupropion, ritalin. Prescription drugs? He didn't know much about
the black market, but he was sure this pill
stash was worth a bundle. There was a

set of papers also. The papers hadn't slid clear when the basement steps creaked. Kenny stepped off the landing and smiled, his gripped knife catching the glare of the bare bulb.

"Kenny..." he started, but he was cut off.

"I heard you did it again. My sister wasn't enough."

"If you'd just listen to me for a..."

He pointed the knife at Beckett's heart. "New plan. You die now, before you can kill anyone else. Then I'll deal with your wife."

Beckett waved the packet. "What I've got in this envelope will show us who really killed Pauline. Rita hid it here, and that's why she was killed too."

"You've always got a story, don't you?" He stepped closer. "It may have convinced the police, but it's not going to help you this time."

"The police are likely on their way here now."

He grinned. "Good. They can mop up

the mess after I split. I told Uncle Leonard to go on ahead. He'll find us a place to start over after I kill you and yours."

At least Uncle Leonard wasn't on the property, ready to pounce on Laney and Irene. Levi would be there by now. Maybe he would figure out something was amiss and call Jude.

Beckett held the envelope at Kenny. "All right. So you're going to kill me. I can't convince you of the truth, but what's it going to hurt to look at what's in here? A minute or two more before I die. What's the harm in it?"

"More time for you to keep breathing."

"One minute more." He paused, his gut wound tight with tension. "You can read, can't you?"

The gibe made Kenny prickle. "You won't look so superior when you're dead. Okay, I'll let you squirm for a while longer. You open it. What's it say?"

Beckett pulled the folded papers from the envelope. There were two sheets, printed screenshots from a computer. Two pictures of the same thing, he thought at first.

Two record sheets with notes, taken after a physical exam. His eyes flew to the top line, the name. No, he had to be wrong. He read it again.

"What does it say?" Kenny said. "Quit stalling."

"I have to get to Laney." Beckett tried to barrel past Kenny, but he lunged forward, the blade sinking into his biceps. He did not feel pain, but blood began to spill down his arm in a warm trickle.

Kenny crouched, gleeful. "Awww. Does it hurt, Beckett?"

The next time Kenny launched an attack, Beckett was ready. He sidestepped and Kenny's momentum carried him forward. Beckett raised his forearm and smashed an elbow into Kenny's chin as he stumbled forward. The strike snapped his head up and he fell to the floor, groaning, the knife popping from his grip and sliding under the shelving unit.

Beckett grabbed the envelope and

sprinted up the stairs, exploding into the kitchen and out to the courtyard. He yelled as he went. "Laney!" But he knew even as he ran to the cabin that he was too late. Levi stood in the doorway, hands on hips, Admiral whining and clattering in anxious circles around the front room. Irene's car was gone.

"I was just about to call you." Levi frowned. "Where's Laney?" He looked closer. "Are you bleeding?"

"Can't explain right now. Kenny's in the basement, semiconscious. Get your rifle. Herm can help you tie him up. I have to go."

"Where?" Levi yelled after him.

To save my wife and my baby.

He leaped into the truck and gunned the motor, dialing as he went. He hadn't finished his own call when his phone lit up with another.

He thumbed it on. "Don't hurt her," he almost shouted.

Irene sounded a million miles away. "Bring me what Rita left, and she'll be fine. I'm going to leave Death Valley and you'll never see me again. I want the papers and the pills. You give them to me and I won't kill her."

"But..." he choked out.

"Drive north from the hotel for ten miles and stop. I'll call you again. No police or she dies."

He was left with a dial tone and his heart beating with such violence he thought his sternum would crack open. Hardly able to breathe, he drove out of the hotel parking lot. Another incoming call sounded from his phone. He stared at the number before he answered.

"Jude, listen."

"What is going on?" his cousin barked. "I just talked to Levi..."

Beckett cut him off. "Dr. Irene killed Pauline to cover up malpractice. Where are you?"

"I'm two minutes from the hotel."

"I need your help."

"I'll..." Jude started.

"Not the Inyo County police department, Jude. You. Please. She has Laney."

There was a heavy silence. He knew his
cousin was measuring their history, the
distrust, the anger and weight of everything that had passed between them since
he'd stepped into the wrestling ring with
Dan all those years ago.

"All right," he said finally. "I'm almost
there."

"No red lights and sirens."

"Beck, if this doesn't work..."

"If it doesn't work, then nothing else
matters."

His answer was clipped, terse. "Copy
that. Wait right there."

And then Beckett pulled to the shoulder,
gripped the steering wheel, counting the
seconds and praying with all his might
that he would get there in time.

Laney felt as though her head was
stuffed full of cotton. Her senses were
numb, slow, cramped as her eyes slowly
opened. She was in the back seat of a car.

Panic exploded as she realized her ankles were bound with duct tape, hands raised above her and zip-tied through the handle intended to help back-seat passengers exit the vehicle.

Irene peered in the rearview mirror.

"Hi, Laney. I hope the ties aren't too tight. I hated to do it, but I didn't want you coming to while I was driving."

"You...drugged me?"

"A mild sedative. Won't hurt the baby, if that's what you're wondering."

She gaped. Could Irene really have drugged and abducted her? She tugged on the wrist binding. "Let me loose."

"When Beckett brings me what I want."

So Rita really had left something at the hotel. "It's proof, isn't it? Proof that you killed Pauline." She could barely believe her own words.

Irene shot a quick look at her in the rearview mirror. "I'm a good doctor."

A good doctor? Had she heard correctly? She peered out the window, trying to gauge how far they were from the hotel. She did not recognize any land-marks. They had diverted course from the main road, traveling one of the thou-sands of isolated trails that crisscrossed Death Valley. Remote trails, where it was unlikely to see another human being for days, perhaps even months. Her mouth went dry. "Yes," she said, distractedly. "A good doctor."

"My father never thought I could do it. I was expelled from high school. I cheated on a test, just one, but they chucked me out anyway. Humiliating. I had to get my GED. But I persevered, in spite of every-thing, got massive student loans and put myself through medical school. It was the best moment in my life when I walked across that stage and they handed me my medical license. You know what my fa-ther said at the ceremony?"

Laney subtly pulled on the handle where her hands were bound, trying to test the sturdiness. "What?"

"He said, *Did you have to cheat on your*

medical boards too?" Irene's lips quivered as she relived the memory.

"I'm sorry," Laney said. "That was unkind." *But it doesn't give you an excuse to kill people.* "But you're right. You're a good doctor."

She shrugged. "Yes, I am. I do pro bono work and go the extra mile to make house calls, don't I?"

"Yes, you do."

"That mistake never should have happened."

The road became bumpy and Laney struggled to keep from bashing against the car door. "What mistake?"

"I was just tired, is all. Trying to squeeze in as many patients as I could in my office in Oregon. There's so much pressure starting a practice, building a clientele, handling staff, insurance, rent, keeping up on training. I'd been short on sleep, living on coffee and fast food." She heaved in a deep breath. "I saw a patient named Cordelia, who presented with abdominal pain. I didn't do a thorough exam because

I was already running an hour behind. I sent her home with a prescription for antacids. I didn't do an ultrasound or blood work. Barely touched her in the physical exam." Irene winced. "She died two days after the appointment from internal bleeding. Pauline was my nurse at the time."

Laney shifted to keep pulling at the handle. Had she felt it give? "Oh, I see now, the Pauline connection."

"The police came calling to question me. I knew I hadn't completed a thorough exam, but I changed the file to say that I'd done a full workup and recommended immediate surgery, but Cordelia declined. The police were satisfied and so was the medical board." She paused. "Pauline knew, though. She realized I'd altered the file. She quit, but not before she saved copies of the file and stole the supply of pills I'd been keeping as an insurance policy. I packed up and fled as soon as the police were done with me. Came to this nowhere to start again."

The handle was definitely loosening.

Laney kept up the pressure, even though the zip tie was cutting into her wrist. "But Pauline found you here, didn't she?"

"Yes, the filthy blackmailer. She had taken screenshots of my initial report and the changed version. The screens were date stamped, proving I'd altered them after the fact. She kept the pills too. I suppose it was too hard for her to sell them herself without getting caught. She tracked me down here and threatened me. Brought the proof, but only one set. She had a second set and my pill stash in a safe place, she said. I didn't have the money to pay her."

"So you killed her?"

"I didn't want to, but she gave me no choice. I needed my stash to fund my getaway, but I couldn't find it, so I hoped no one else would either. I figured with Pauline dead, maybe I'd be okay here for a while."

Incredulity warred with Laney's disgust. The woman she'd trusted with her health and her baby's. How could she have been so blind? "You let Beckett take the blame. No, you framed him by writing the note and putting Pauline's sweater in his car. You sent him to jail, enabled Kenny to terrorize both of us. You never said a word."

"I am sorry. I like Beckett and I like you. If I could have figured another way, I'd have taken it, but I couldn't run again, not then. I have some money saved up now. And when Beckett brings me the pills, I'll have plenty."

Laney thought back over the last harrowing weeks. "The snake? Throwing rocks at me at the spring? I can't believe you did those things."

"I didn't. I imagine that was Kenny, but it worked in my favor. Kenny really is a bad dude, you know."

Laney felt like crying, but she gulped back her emotions as Irene continued.

"When you told me Rita was investigating Pauline's death, possibly looking for some sort of proof she was murdered, I couldn't believe it. I tried to scare her, with the fire. I guess I did, but she got me in the end anyway, hiding my package in your basement."

The bolt that fastened the handle to the roof of the car began to shimmy. She pulled harder, trying to keep the effort out of her voice. "What happened with Rita? You killed her too, didn't you?"

Irene shook her head. "There's no more time to talk about that right now. We're here."

Laney stared out into the blackness. "Where?"

Irene pulled off a dirt track into a hollow surrounded by hills. "I love running, you know. Sometimes I run for most of the night while it's cool. I find all kinds of things."

She got out.

Laney tugged frantically, but the bolt refused to give. Tears crowded her eyes, her wrists stung, but she could not free herself.

Irene came around to Laney's door and opened it, pulling a pair of clippers from her pocket. "I'm going to cut you loose."

Laney's heart beat faster.

Irene snipped the zip tie. Laney got out of the car.

"Come on," Irene said, gesturing to the darkness.

"My ankles… I can't walk."

"Hop, then."

Laney stared. How could this be the same woman who she'd believed was her friend? Confidante? "You took an oath," she said. "To do no harm."

Irene stopped. "Yes, I did, but in order to follow my oath, I have to continue practicing medicine, don't I? It will be easier for me when I've got my pills. I can pay for a new identity and start over."

"This is not what you vowed to do."

Irene pulled a small gun from her pocket. "I don't have time. I have to meet Beckett."

Ice formed in Laney's belly. "What are you going to do to him?"

"Nothing, if he gives me what I want. Then I'll take off and call him to tell him where you are."

Her tone was overly casual, a shade too bright. Laney realized it would be simpler for Irene if Laney and Beckett did not live to tell the police what they knew. Rita was dead and so was Pauline. Laney's and Beckett's murders might be pinned on Kenny, and Dr. Irene would cease to exist in favor of another identity. She swallowed a rising tide of terror as they came to an old ruin, a cement pier supporting a rusting eight-foot-tall pole. It was the remnants of some sort of mining machinery, common to Death Valley. Irene had made sure they were well away from the road, concealed by the rippling hills. No one would see them there. Laney was still alive just to make sure Beckett cooperated. And then…

Make a plan, she ordered herself. She figured her only way to get to Beckett was to wait until Irene left and take off on foot, but how could she get anywhere with her ankles taped together? She'd need to come up with a better scheme than that.

She didn't get the chance.

"Hands behind you, back to the pole."

"What? Why?"

"Do it."

"And if I don't?"

She pointed the gun at Laney's belly. "Please don't make me."

A ball of terror exploded, leaving her dizzy. Her baby...their baby. She had no choice but to comply. Hardly able to draw breath, she backed up to the pole and Irene fastened zip ties around her wrists, securing her to the pole.

"I figure Beckett might need proof that you're okay before he hands over the stuff. If he forces my hand, I'll bring him close enough to see you before..."

Before she killed him, then her.

"Don't hurt Beckett," she screamed as Irene walked away. "Haven't you done enough to him already?"

Irene stopped for a moment. Then she continued to walk away without looking back.

NINETEEN

Jude pulled on a rubber glove, reading from the note Rita had fastened to the papers.

Beckett,
I am sorry. I decided I don't want to be involved anymore. I will call you to tell you where I hid this packet, but if something goes wrong, I hope you'll find it.
The short story is, I ran into Pauline by chance at the drugstore in our hometown. She was photocopying papers, worried, stressed. They spilled all over the floor and she scooped them up and ran. I got only a peek while I helped her gather them, enough to see a doctor's name and make out

that it was screenshots of a chart, two copies of each. I didn't think much of it, but when Pauline was murdered, I paid closer attention. I wondered if she'd copied two sets of that screenshot before she confronted whoever killed her; blackmail, I guessed, with a dose of caution.

No papers or photos were found in her possession or her home, according to the police, so that made me think she'd stashed them someplace. What better location than a tiny hotel in the middle of a great big desert? I already told you I had dreams of becoming the hotshot reporter, breaking the Pauline Sanderson story wide open. Well, I found the papers, all right, behind the wardrobe in Pauline's room, plus a bonus supply of prescription drugs I assume to be destined for the black market. I knew Doc Irene was the killer. Who would have thought that?

I was on my way to show you the bundle when I overheard you two tell-

ing Irene that you thought I was looking for the proof. I lost my nerve right
then. I am sure Irene caused the fire
in my hotel room. That was enough
for me. Between Kenny and Irene, I
am hanging up my investigative hat.
Hopefully, I will be calling you with
this info. If not, then I hope you will
find it someday on your own. You
don't deserve what happened to you.
Neither did Pauline.
Rita

Jude shook his head. "Rita didn't make
it out of town fast enough. Irene must have
driven her off the road after she left the
auto shop."

"That would explain why Irene missed
her morning appointments."

"Forced her into her trunk and re-
strained her somehow, but she managed
to get that call out to you. Later that night,
Irene drove her to the woods and killed
her, left her car there and your hat."

Jude took photos of the papers and the

pills, eased them back into the envelope and slid it into a plastic bag from his back pocket. When he laid it on the seat, Beckett snatched it up.

Jude frowned and offered a manila envelope instead. He grabbed some old maps from Beckett's truck and shoved them inside. "The heft will fool her for a few moments. Figured you wouldn't want to hand over the real proof, right? The pictures are only a backup. We'll want the originals and the pills to make the case against her."

"If she suspects, she might bolt without telling us where Laney is."

Jude stared out the window at the long, flat road ahead. "Beck, you know that Irene might have killed her already."

"No," he grated out. "I don't believe that. I can't. Laney is her insurance that I will hand over the packet."

"I need you to be prepared. We cannot hand over this proof. If we do, two murders might go unpunished."

And possibly a third and fourth, if Irene

killed Laney and the baby. He gritted his teeth.

"I've got the park police on standby," Jude added. "If Irene gets away, we'll dispatch search teams and helicopters. They'll find Laney. It's what they do."

He shook his head. "I will give Irene anything she wants to protect my wife and baby."

"You can't do that. Unless we get that proof, you'll never be free of suspicion."

"I don't care. They have to live and thrive. That's it. That's all."

"They will," he said quietly.

If it isn't too late already, Beckett read in his tone. His phone buzzed and he snatched it.

"I'll meet you on the Salt Pan trail," Irene said. "Turn off your car and get out and stand in the middle of the path. You'd better be alone."

"I want to talk to…"

"Do it." The connection ended.

Beckett felt dizzy with fear.

"That location gives her easy access to

the main road," Jude said. "She's probably planning to kill you both and take off, not stick around and let Laney go."

"Her plan's gonna change." His body felt as though it was slowly becoming stone. He could endure anything, survive any pain or physical trauma, whatever, if Laney and the baby lived.

Jude held out a palm. "Beck, you have to give me the proof."

Beckett shook his head. "Do what you have to, Jude. Arrest me—this time I deserve it maybe for disobeying the law, but I am asking you to give me the chance to save my family. Will you give me that, cousin?"

The only sound for a long moment was the wind blowing grit against the windshield. Jude shifted in his seat and rubbed a hand across his eyes. "There's a turn just before the trail where I can get out without her seeing. I'll circle around, get behind her if I can."

Beckett sighed. "Thank you." He pushed the truck through the restless night.

Hold on, Laney. I'll be there soon, honey. He drove rapidly, pushing the speed limit except for the ten-second stop just before the trail where Jude leaped out and disappeared into the night. Beckett kept on, mind whirling. He would string Irene along, keep her there until Jude could get into position. She would not get away and she would not be able to hurt Laney...unless she already had.

The thought would have rendered him immobile, if he actually could make himself believe it, but his soul would not allow it. God would not take her and his baby. Even if he was not ever to really be her husband again, God would not end their story that way. He clung to that with the desperation of a man dangling over a cliff, holding the fraying ends of a rope.

His phone buzzed again.

"I can see your headlights. Turn right in fifty yards and stay on the phone," Irene said.

He did, the truck rattling over the ground.

"Shut off the engine and stand in the

path and keep your hands where I can see them."

He killed the ignition and a set of headlights blinked on, blinding him. His eyes adjusted to make out the figure of Irene, arm outstretched and aiming a pistol.

"Give it to me," she said.

"Where's Laney?"

"Close by."

"Not good enough."

"It will have to be."

"It's not, Irene. I have no reason to trust you. You killed two people and abducted your patient."

He heard her breath hiss out. "I don't have time to explain it. Give it to me. Now."

He saw a flicker of movement behind her. Jude?

"I want to know where my wife…" He didn't get the sentence finished before she pulled the trigger. A bullet whizzed by his temple. Reflexively, he hunched down, pulse hammering.

"I'm an excellent shot and I can search

your dead body just as well as your live one. I'm going to ask you one more time and then I will kill you. I will drive from this spot to where Laney is and kill her too. Then I will leave here with the packet or without. Your only chance to save what you love is to give me what I want. That's it. No negotiating."

Still no Jude. If he gave her the packet, she would likely shoot him anyway. Jude would find Laney. In what condition?

Slowly he pulled the envelope from where he'd tucked it under his shirt.

What choice did he have?

None at all.

Blood trickled down Laney's wrists. There was no point in yanking against the zip tie that bound her to the pole. She had to figure out another way. The fleeting patches of moonlight were not enough to illuminate the cloud-swept sky. Any moment Beckett might be arriving at the rendezvous with Irene.

"All right, girlfriend," she muttered

aloud. "You're gonna have to get out of this all by yourself."

She looked up at the tip of the rusted pole. It stretched some three feet above her head. There was no way she could climb to the top, even if she weren't tied in place. Willow, Beckett's extremely athletic cousin, could probably have done it, but not under the present circumstances. She raised her hands as far as she could behind her back, and her probing fingers encountered a place where a protruding hinge had corroded, leaving a sharp metal edge.

An impractical plan formed in her mind, but she did not allow herself to think of the yawning possibility of failure. She slid down the pole to the ground and used her taped feet to scoop as much gritty soil as she could into a pile. Standing on it, she realized the pile wasn't high enough—she still could not reach the sharp spot, so she sank down and scraped more. Her thighs ached and her shins cramped. Panting and sweating, she crafted her hard-won debris into a taller mound. Carefully, she climbed to her feet again, stood on the pile and slid her arms up the pole.

Now her wrists were just even with the roughened metal. Immediately, she began to saw away at the zip tie. The position was excruciating on her muscles and she had to stop several times to rest. After five minutes of determined sawing, she began to despair. Maybe her plan would not work.

But five minutes had become ten, maybe fifteen since Irene had left. She was running out of time. Another round of backbreaking contortions, and she felt the glorious sensation of the zip tie giving way to the rusted metal hinge. She kept sawing.

When she thought she could not sustain the effort one more moment, one wrist came free. Now she was able to turn and apply herself to sawing away the other manacle. When she finished, she collapsed on the ground, sweating.

You have to find him, warn him. She

had to get back to the main road and that would be challenge enough in the dark. With her fingernails, she found the seam of the duct tape and unwound it from her ankles. She stood painfully, pushing past the muscle cramps, wishing her eyes would adjust like Beckett always said they would. Walking only a few steps, she tumbled and went to her knees. Muttering, she got up again.

How was she going to get back to the main road without breaking a limb? She shoved her hands into the pockets of her sweater, pulled out the lighter. Stripping off her sweater, she found several long, dry sticks. Bundling them up, she used the duct tape from her ankles and secured the sweater in a tight knot around the top. "Too bad. I really liked this sweater."

She lit the bunched sweater with her lighter and it began to burn, along with the duct tape. It wouldn't provide light for long, but maybe it would get her back to the road.

She half walked, half jogged, the light

flickering from the stick as her sweater burned. It was not enough to keep her from stumbling, but she soldiered on in the direction of the main road. Bits of sweater now reduced to ash fell from the makeshift torch. How long would the fuel hold out?

Pushing onward, she held the light in front of her, ignoring the sting of smoke in her eyes.

Time was running out for Beckett. *Hurry, Laney.*

Beckett held the envelope and Irene stepped forward to take it, but she leaned out, making sure he could not lunge forward and grab her. The gun was aimed steadily as she pried the envelope open and peered inside.

"All right. Did you take anything out?"

"No."

"I'm going to assume you're telling the truth. You wouldn't risk your wife and baby just to send me to jail."

"You deserve to be there." As soon as he said it, he wished he hadn't.

"No," she snapped. "I'm a good doctor, like I told your wife. She knows I am. I took excellent care of her and the baby."

When you weren't killing people and framing others for murder. This time he didn't vocalize the thoughts. "Where's Laney?"

Irene backed up several steps toward her car. "I'll call you."

Rage reared inside him like a runaway horse. "You're not leaving here without telling me."

She fired again. The shot would have taken his head off if he hadn't dived to the side. He scrambled to his feet to run after her when Jude crested the nearest foothill. "Police! Freeze, Irene."

She fired.

Jude returned fire. The bullet missed, but she recoiled backward, falling hard into the front of her car. Beckett heard the thunk of her skull against the metal bumper. She collapsed, unmoving.

He ran to her.

"Stay back, Beckett," Jude shouted.

Irene lay on her side, breathing, but unconscious.

Jude elbowed him out of the way. "Ambulance and park rangers are already rolling." He checked her pulse. "She's alive."

"She didn't tell me," Beckett panted, panic consuming him. "I don't know where Laney is."

"We'll find her."

He whirled away, running to the main road. The asphalt stretched endlessly in both directions. Behind him lay the network of wilderness, acres of desert. He turned in a helpless circle. Which way should he look?

Sirens wailed as the ambulance and park service vehicles roared up, personnel running to assist Jude with the fallen woman. Everything seemed so far off, removed from his stream of consciousness. His hands balled into fists and terror almost stopped his breathing. He couldn't move, couldn't talk. He was not even sure his heart still beat. Nothing mattered, nothing at all but Laney, his wife, his love, the mother of his baby.

"Laney!" His shout bounced along the road, echoing cruelly back at him.

What if she was lying hurt, suffering, afraid?

But a worse alternative presented itself to him that almost made his knees buckle.

Officers were moving toward him, he realized. They would start the search party, fan out and do what they did, as Jude said. What would they find?

"Laney," he shouted one more time.

Only the wind replied.

His vision narrowed, gloom tunneling in, until a glimmer of light appeared on the road in the distance. It flickered and danced as if it was one of those tiki torches Laney insisted on at the hotel. He blinked. The glimmer remained, growing closer. Was he imagining it? He realized it was a torch, almost out, but with a weak glow that outlined a delicate arm holding it aloft.

His mouth fell open.

A hallucination?

But the figure drew close enough that everything stopped, his breathing, his movement, his power of speech, his ability to see anything around him except that God-given sight.

Laney walked closer, limping. Her clothes were torn and filthy. Then the paralysis ended and he launched himself along the road.

She dropped the strange torch she carried and it snuffed out. In less than a minute, he'd gathered her into his arms. For a moment, he could not make words, as he caged her in an embrace, his cheek pressed to her smoky hair, fingers feeling the heaving of her body as she cried.

"Are you injured?" he finally choked out, trying to move her to arm's length.

She would not allow him to move her from his chest. "We are okay," she sobbed. "Are you?"

He simply could not answer.

"Is Irene…?"

"Jude has her and the packet Rita hid. It's over. It's all over." He said it as much to convince himself as her. The crimes were solved and his reputation might be shored up, but there was no room in his soul for anything but the most profound gratitude to God for saving Laney and the baby.

TWENTY

Laney insisted Beckett accompany her in the ambulance to the hospital. "Otherwise, I'm not going," she announced to the paramedics. Jude gestured that he should be allowed. She could not stop crying, for some reason, as the medics took her vitals and checked her over. All her overextended muscles would hurt like gangbusters in the morning, she had no doubt. On the way, her mind was a jumble of fragmented thoughts.

Irene was in custody, and she would never hurt anyone again.

But it was too late for Pauline and Rita.

"Kenny..." she whispered through cracked lips.

Beckett stroked her hand. "He's under

arrest. Levi and Herm took care of things perfectly."

"And…"

"And Willow is staying with Admiral so he won't be alone tonight." He kissed her fingertips. "You don't need to be worried about anything, honey."

"As long as the baby's all right," she finished.

He cast a longing glance at her blanket-covered tummy. Guiding his hand, she clasped it atop her belly, sandwiching it beneath hers. "But I think you're right. Muffin is tough," she said.

"Like her mother."

"Or his."

"Either one is fine with me."

She looked sharply at him. "You still look sad. Why?"

He shrugged. "Nothing… I…" He exhaled. "Someone once told me sharing feelings is everything." He cleared his throat. "I was wondering if any of this news will change minds in town."

"Some people will always see you as

a bad guy, Beckett. The question is, do you?"

He was silent, staring at his hand placed on her stomach. Before he had time to answer, they were whisked into the local clinic. This time, no one had suggested a helicopter ride to Las Vegas. "Beckett, will you...?" she started to ask as she was rolled into the examining room. His big frame crowded the doorway and she knew it was a silly question. He wouldn't leave her, unless she asked him to keep the promise he'd made to her earlier.

Should she? Shouldn't she? The echo of betrayal still sounded deep in her soul somewhere, like a badly played note. Ah, but the other notes, the music that had grown watching him change, to grow into the man God meant him to be... Didn't that drown out the rest? Suddenly she was too tired to think anymore, and she closed her eyes and let the doctor finish the exam without her help. She awakened just long enough to hear about "strained tendons, pulled muscles, mild dehydration, abrasions," but all that fell by the wayside when she heard the last bit.

"The baby is just fine, Mr. Duke," the doctor said.

Too tired to open her eyes, she let the tears leak down her cheeks until someone whisked them away with a tissue. She did not need to see to know who it was.

"I want to go home." Laney did not want to talk about anything, it seemed to Beckett. There was something weighing on her. Residual trauma from the abduction? Physical discomfort? He drove her back to the hotel. Her brows were drawn together, and even his suggestion to supply her and Muffin with a milkshake did not bring more than a polite "no, thank you."

Uncertainty stripped him of confidence. He knew what he had to do, had to ask, but now he was not at all sure of the answer he would receive. At the hotel, he looped Laney's arm in his as he guided her through the lodge, where Dan Wheatly greeted them with a smile and news. His assistant stood with him.

"Irene is being charged with the murders of Pauline and Rita. Kenny is also being booked. It will take some more convincing for him to believe that you aren't to blame, Beckett. The cops got Uncle Leonard too. Jude said to tell you he will be here later. I'm on my way to the station to make sure the paperwork is all in order."

"Thank you," Beckett said. The two men shook hands.

Willow launched herself out of the cabin as they approached, Admiral yipping joyfully as he tried to keep up. She hugged both Beckett and Laney at once, pulling them close and squealing. "You're okay. You're both okay." She repeated it over and over until they managed to detach themselves.

"I promised I'd tell Aunt Kitty the moment I clapped eyes on you, but I'll bring dinner."

Beckett smiled. "It's ten thirty in the morning."

"Oh. Breakfast, then. Scones."

"When was the last time you made scones?" Laney asked.

"Never, but Aunt Kitty makes great ones. I'll go fill her in and we'll return with baskets full of food. Promise." She smacked a kiss on both their cheeks.

Laney sighed. "I think we are about to be buried in piles of carbohydrate comfort."

He pushed open the door and held it as she entered. "Worse things could happen."

Admiral was panting and wheezing, so she lifted him tenderly onto his cushion on the sofa.

And then they were alone. His palms went clammy.

"Laney, um, do you want to sit down?"

"No," she said with a groan. "My back is complaining from the ride."

He was about to suggest she lie down and let him fetch her an ice pack when she turned to him.

"I'm not sure what to do from here." She blinked. "All of a sudden this is awkward, isn't it?"

Torture, was more like it. He cleared his throat. "I need to say something, and then I'll go if you want me to."

She cocked her head, sending hair tumbling across her brow. He longed to touch it.

"I've messed up everything in my life since high school. I can't undo some of the damage, and maybe I'll always have people whispering behind my back."

She pressed her lips together and he could not read her thoughts for anything. Shifting, he started again. "You and Muffin... I mean, you deserve a husband and daddy you can be proud of. I want to be that man, but I don't know... I mean, I'm not sure you can grow to feel that way again, like you did before."

Still she did not answer.

"I love you," he said. Her mouth pinched tight, and she looked down.

"I thought I knew who I was and what

love meant. I didn't. Love is…" His voice broke. "Love is when someone is ready to stand by you in the worst moments of your life. You were willing to do that for me then and now. I never knew how strong you could be, but your love is made of steel."

She still didn't answer.

"I don't know if it's too late, Laney. I promised I'd leave you alone, but I'm going to ask one more time. If you say no, I will honor that, support you and the baby from afar." He gulped. "I love you. You make me better. You've shown me what it means to put everything on the line for someone. You taught me what it means to love for better or worse. I've given you worse, but I promise, I want to give you and the baby better."

She bit her lip. In anger? Forgiveness? Dismissal?

Abruptly, she turned on her heel and left him to go into the bedroom. He wondered if she would slam the door, shut him out of her life.

Beckett, you don't get a second chance. Not this time. He closed his eyes, trying to keep breathing, to summon the strength to walk out the door and away from where God had meant for him to be.

She returned, her face unreadable. She thrust something out and he held up a palm. Into it, she dropped a plain gold band, her wedding ring. The pain was worse than the beating he'd taken in jail. She was giving it back to him...too little, too late.

"I'm sorry," he whispered.

"Beckett?"

He looked at her. "I understand. I made a promise and I will keep it. You don't have to explain anything to me."

"Apparently, I do. I think what you are asking requires another formal request, don't you?"

He stared, unable to fathom her half smile.

"Ask me," she said, a tremor in her voice.

"What?"

She pointed to the ring. "Ask me."

He looked at the ring and at her. He saw it then, warmth, forgiveness, tenderness and strength all wrapped up in that smile, and those eyes, and that woman.

He knelt, holding the ring gently, as if it might bend under his touch. Hardly able to push past the emotion, he half whispered. "Laney, will you still be my wife?"

She held up her fingers and he slid it on. Her hands were shaking, just a little. "Yes, Beckett. I love you and Muffin will love you too. We will always be your family, and I will always be your wife."

He leaped to his feet, gathering his wife and his baby in one enormous hug and lifting them up.

Admiral added his excited yelp to the celebration.

Elation, pure and simple, flowed out of him. He set her down but held her close. "It may be a struggle for the hotel, take some time to build back up the business, but..."

She wrapped her arms around his neck.

"But you'll have plenty of time to fix up a nursery for Muffin while things are slow."

"Yes, ma'am." He marveled at her, pressing kisses to her temple, her cheeks, her lips. He had his wife back, and what was more, he would soon experience parenting. He gulped.

"What's wrong?"

"I guess it just hit me, the whole fatherhood thing. I need to learn all about how to do it properly. Maybe read some books. Or, uh, I mean, what should I do first?"

With her fingertips, she smoothed the frown that puckered his brow. "That's easy."

He looked at her in astonishment. "It is?"

"Uh-huh. I'm very close to Muffin, you know. We have a connection. The most important thing right now is to make Muffin a big pile of pancakes."

He threw back his head and whooped with laughter. "With extra syrup?"

"Tons."

He felt the last fetter that bound his heart

drop away, just as God had always meant for it to do.

"I love you, Laney."

"I love you too. So let's go see about those pancakes, Daddy."

Daddy. He laughed again with the pure delight of it. "Yes, let's," he said.

* * * * *

If you enjoyed this story,
look for these other books
by Dana Mentink:

Danger on the Ranch
Deadly Christmas Pretense
Cold Case Connection
Secrets Resurfaced

Dear Reader,

Don't you just love fiction? My favorite part is that I get to dish up a big fat happy ending. It's not like that in life, is it? I am writing this letter during our tenth week of sheltering in place. I am sure your life has been turned upside down too. My college kiddos are trying to finish up online. Folks worldwide are struggling to figure out how to navigate sudden unemployment, missing friends and family, and disconnection from our communities. Throughout it all, I am reminded that God's love is so deep and wide that it transcends all the difficulties of this world. I hope you find comfort in knowing that nothing is a surprise to Him. He sees us, He knows us, He loves us, all of us, all the time.

As always, you can reach me via my website, Facebook and Twitter, or you can reach out with a letter to PO Box 3168 San Ramon, CA 94583. May God richly bless you, friends.

Yours truly,

Dana Mentink